Praise for Alena and Wynter Pitts and the
Lena in the Spotlight Series

"Tween girls LOVE fiction, but it doesn't always teach them the best values. That's why I'm so excited about Wynter Evans Pitts writing with her daughter Alena. This is a book series that will entertain your daughter's love of reading, but also introduce godly living. Enjoy!"

—DANNAH GRESH

"Alena Pitts is an absolute treasure! She and her parents have a heart for ministry and for advancing God's kingdom. One of the best decisions we made in casting for the movie *War Room* was in choosing Alena to be Danielle. She not only brought an outstanding performance to the film, but she and her family were a joy to work with. We can look forward to great things from this little world changer."

—STEPHEN KENDRICK

Every little girl dreams and Alena Pitts has written a delightful book series that will help any girl do just that. Taking a cue from her own life as a young actress, Alena weaves a story that will take her reader on a fun adventure while simultaneously encouraging her to both dream and keep first things first. The concepts of faith, family, and following your dreams are all laced together into a tale that is sure to keep any girl turning the pages while she also learns life lessons and is reminded of God's love.

—CHRYSTAL EVANS HURST CO-AUTHOR OF *KINGDOM WOMAN*

Shining Night

Other Books by Alena Pitts with Wynter Pitts

Lena in the Spotlight Series

Hello Stars (Book One)

Day Dreams and Movie Screens (Book Two)

LENA IN THE SPOTLIGHT

Shining Night

BY ALENA PITTS

WITH WYNTER PITTS

ZONDERKIDZ

Shining Night
Copyright © 2018 by Alena Pitts and Wynter Pitts
Illustrations © 2018 by Zondervan

This title is also available as a Zondervan ebook.

Requests for information should be addressed to:
Zonderkidz, *3900 Sparks Dr. SE, Grand Rapids, Michigan 49546*

ISBN 978-0-310-76061-0

Cover illustration: Annabelle Matayer
Interior illustration: Jacqui Davis
Interior design: Denise Froehlich

Printed in the United States of America

18 19 20 21 22 /LSC/ 10 9 8 7 6 5 4 3 2 1

Auntie Silla, I love you!
Alena

"Lena! There is a package for you!" Amber was standing in the middle of the kitchen floor staring at me. She was holding a brown box and flashing a toothless grin. After a long day at school I was excited to finally be home. I carefully used my one free hand to push through the door.

I released my lunchbox from my two front teeth and let it fall to the floor. Followed by my backpack, grey sweatshirt, water bottle, and the blue and orange history book that Ms. Blount forced me to bring home. I let out a deep sigh. It felt good to have the use of both my hands and mouth once again.

"Can I open it? Please, please, please?" Amber's grin widened as she begged, teasingly shaking the box right in front of my face.

"Nope!" I leaned forward and pretended I was going to grab it out of her hands. Instead I reached both arms out and tickled her belly until she had no choice but to loosen her grip on the box and let me have it.

"Okay, Lena!" She tried to catch her breath as she placed the box in my hands.

I took one look at it and squealed, "It's from Mallory!"

Mom heard the commotion and walked into the kitchen with a curious look on her face. When she saw me holding the box, she smiled.

"Hi, Lena. How was school?" she asked. "I see you got

your package. Did you see that it's from Mallory?" she added.

"I did! I wonder what it is," I said.

"Open it *after* you get all your things up off the floor!" Mom sneakily grabbed the package from my hands without even giving me a chance to stop her.

My eyes popped open wide with surprise and my mouth dropped open. "Mom!" I squealed playfully.

She and Amber exchanged a high-five and giggled.

"Gotcha!"

She was tickled by her ability to move so quickly.

Mom placed the package on the table and headed toward the refrigerator.

"Girls, come get your snack!" she called out for Ansley and Ashton to join us in the kitchen. Normally, after-school snacks are my favorite, but today I was much more interested in finding out what was in that box!

I hurried to pick up everything I'd dropped just a few moments ago.

Ansley came running into the kitchen carrying Austin, one arm wrapped tightly around his belly. Austin was wearing a red bandana around his left paw. He looked helpless yet happy with his legs loosely dangling near Ansley's waist. Amber marched behind her wearing her light blue pretend doctor's coat with a white and red plastic stethoscope hanging from her neck. It suddenly made sense. My sisters were playing veterinarian and Austin was, of course, the sick puppy. I smiled.

"Hey, guys."

"Hey, Lena. Did you see your big box?"

"Yup! I'm going to open it in a second."

I rustled Austin's fur a little and tossed my water bottle and entire lunchbox into the sink. *I'll empty it later,* I thought to myself. I grabbed my backpack, sweatshirt, and textbook, and ran them down the hall to my bedroom. I threw it all right on top of my unmade bed and three-day old socks and pajamas. *Ohhh, I should clean up before Mom sees this.* I thought about cleaning it up for a second but decided I didn't want to wait any longer to see what Mallory had sent. I headed back to the kitchen instead.

"Can I open it now, Mom?" I asked, with one hand already tugging at the tape on the side.

Mom nodded and smiled.

Amber, Ashton, Ansley, and even Austin gathered around and waited with excitement as I wrestled with the box until it was finally open enough for us to see a glittery blue box hiding inside.

"It's . . . another box!" Amber announced.

Once the blue box was completely free, I could see a tiny white envelope attached to it with three pieces of flowery printed tape. My name was printed in large purple bubble letters across the top.

"It's so cute!" my sisters and I squealed.

Mom peeked over our shoulders and said, "Aww, yes, it is."

"Come on, Lena, open it!" Ansley demanded.

I pulled the card up close to my chest and paused. With four sets of eyes staring at me, and Austin nibbling on my kneecaps, it suddenly felt like maybe I should open the note in private where I could concentrate better.

Mallory had been such a good friend to me. Almost like a big sister. I always took her advice seriously, but I wasn't sure how having to leave the tour so suddenly had affected our friendship. When my grandmother got sick, I knew she understood that it was an emergency. But even though she was sympathetic, I still felt bad. She had done so much to make sure that Mom and I and our entire family were comfortable on the road with her. Everything from our own tour bus to the special snacks and treats at each of the venues we appeared. It all seemed like a waste now.

Mom had offered to have me go back once we knew that my grandmother was going to be okay, but Mallory insisted that we stay home and spend time with our family. She'd told me she was really close with her grandmother too, and she understood how scary it could be when they get sick. She even called a few times to pray with us. And when we told her that everything was going to be okay, she cheered, "Thank you, Jesus!" on the other end of the phone.

There was no doubt that she cared about the family, but I had not heard from her since then.

That was at least a month ago.

I couldn't help but wonder why she was reaching out now and not just with a phone call or an email but with a big package.

"Well, Lena. Open it!" Ansley interrupted my thoughts.

I let out a deep breath and opened it.

The notecard was even smaller than the envelope and the front and back were covered in Mallory's handwriting.

"She writes so pretty!" Amber acknowledged.

"She writes a lot," Ashton blurted out.

We all agreed with both.

I stood quietly and read each word on the front side to myself.

When I finished, I could feel the curiosity building in each of my sisters, so I read it again, out loud this time, before flipping to the back.

Dear Ms. Lena Daniels, ☺

Hey girl! How is life? Sorry I have not been in touch lately, but things have been busy. I am working on some new music! Can't wait for you to hear it. Well, the tour ended with a great finish. Since you had to leave, we decided to just play a scene from the movie and a little clip from the first interview we did together! That seems like so long ago now. Can you believe how well the movie is doing? Mr. Fenway says he thinks we will be nominated for an award! How crazy would that be? Whenever I think about it, I am so grateful that you sent your tape in to audition even if you had red goo stuck on your teeth! I just love how you never let your fears stop you from trying something new. Never stop doing that. Doing something, even when we are afraid, is what it means to have courage. Lena Daniels, you are one courageous girl! God has given you some-thing beautiful to share and I pray you never forget that. Always be willing to tell others about Him. I love thinking about how He showed His love for you during the filming of Above the Waters, *on* tour as you stood on stage in front of thousands of strangers, and at home while you are loving on your grandmother and family!

This is only the beginning for you, my friend!

I flipped the card over and continued to read.

I wanted you to know that I'm still praying for your grandmother—that God would continue to give her strength and help her to stay healthy! I want to meet her one day soon!

I also wanted you to know that I miss you so much! I hope this box of goodies makes you smile. I thought carefully about everything I included. I think you will know what they all mean, so I won't explain!

There is one thing that I included that I do want to talk to you about. You'll know when you see it.

We will catch up again soon!

Love, Mallory

When I finished reading, no one said a word. They were either not impressed with Mallory's note or so curious to see what was actually inside of the mysterious box that they could not think of anything to say.

I think it was the curiosity that kept them quiet because as soon I lifted the top off the blue box everyone gasped with excitement!

The first thing I spotted was a white sweatshirt just like the one Mallory was wearing when she visited our family! Ashton held it up high and immediately asked Mom if she could get one.

Right under the sweatshirt was a plastic zipper bag with a pack of gum and a pair of scissors. Mom laughed really hard when she saw this. She remembered our first meeting with Mallory in the airport bathroom as she tried to get that gum out of my hair!

After that I spotted a roll of toilet paper and a pair of black sunglasses. I chuckled. Mallory knew how often I ran to the restroom to cry when I was afraid or nervous, so I assume she wanted me to be well-stocked for whatever my next adventure would be! I guessed the sunglasses were to hide my red eyes.

"Did she send these for us?" Ansley asked while glancing in the box at the four giant-sized packs of fruit snacks attached to a bundle of CDs.

"Yup! I think so!" I said.

Ansley, Ashton, and Amber each grabbed their bundle and immediately asked Mom if they could open them.

Now that we had practically cleared out the box, I could see that there were a few photos lying at the bottom. There was a picture of Mallory and me on stage, another of my mom, dad, and sisters sitting on the tour bus together with our driver, and a few more with new friends from the different places we visited. Each one made me smile. Looking at them brought back so many memories of the tour. But the last photo was the one I was least expecting.

There was a picture of Caroline, one of the little girls

Mallory and I met when we visited the children's hospital in Tennessee. As soon as I saw it my eyes filled with tears. I could tell this was not just a fun picture to bring back memories. It looked important. I held it up to get a closer look. Attached to the back of the picture was an official looking card with information about Caroline: her birthday, her favorite games to play, and her favorite foods. Below that were the words—*Want to help sponsor me?*

"Mom!" I shouted. "What does this mean?"

Mom took the card and turned it over to read the information.

"Do you know her?" she asked.

"Yes! I met her when Mallory and I visited the children's hospital. Remember I stuffed an outfit in my backpack because I felt like I was supposed to give it to a little girl?"

Mom nodded slowly, remembering.

"That's her! Caroline is the little girl I gave my outfit to. Why does she need a sponsor? Can I do it?"

Mom flipped the card back over and looked up at me with concern in her eyes.

"Well, Lena, it looks like she needs help to pay for the medical treatment she has been getting. The other side of this card with her personal information has more details. Sounds like the hospital has lost funding and is closing. Probably all of the children need help of some sort."

"I want to help her!" I shouted.

"Yeah, let's help her!" Amber agreed.

"Well, girls, medical treatment can be very expensive. Let's talk to Dad when he gets home. We can help her, but I am afraid she may need more than we have to give."

"We have to do something . . ." I could feel my eyes filling with tears. "We have to help her."

Mom looked helpless and wrapped her arms around me. Ansley, Amber, and Ashton each wrapped their arms around my waist. We stood quietly for a few more seconds in a group hug.

"We will do something," Mom spoke softly.

Just then Austin announced Dad's arrival with a few loud yelps. He ran to the back door, stood up on his back two legs, and began licking the glass. He dropped down to his belly for a few seconds before jumping up again and repeating this cycle several times until Dad finally walked through the door.

"Dad's home early today!" Amber said with a huge smile. She and Ashton ran to greet him.

Ansley darted toward the kitchen table and grabbed her fruit snacks and CD.

Dad had barely set one foot in the door before Ansley started shouting, "Daddy! Daddy! Look what Mallory sent us!"

"Hey, guys! Aww, is that her newest CD? That's great." Dad's face was bright. He loved all the attention he got when he returned from being gone all day.

"Hi, babe," Mom said while reaching over Austin, Ansley, Amber, and Ashton for a hug.

I waited patiently for my turn.

"Hey, Lena," he said and wrapped an arm around my shoulders. As soon as I laid my head on his chest I could feel the tears starting to come. I wanted to wait to tell him about the hospital, but I couldn't.

"Daddy," I said softly while trying to hold on to my emotions.

"What's going on, Lena? What's wrong?"

Everyone stood still and listened as I retold every detail about meeting Caroline while we were on tour, her sickness, Mallory's box, and my broken heart.

As I talked, Dad's face softened.

"Let's call Mallory. We can get more information about what is happening with the hospital, Caroline, and her family. Then we will see how we can help."

"Can we call now?" I begged.

"Maybe we should wait a little bit. Daddy just walked in," Mom said.

"It's okay. We can try now." Dad gave Mom a little shrug as if to say, "Let's get it done so we can eat dinner in peace."

I felt a tiny smile come to my face as Dad pulled out his phone and called Mallory.

He put the phone on speaker and we all stood anxiously as it rang.

Finally, we heard Mallory's voice, but it was only her voicemail. After the beep, Dad said, "Hi, Mallory, it's the Daniels family. We are all here on speaker . . . We got your package today. Thank you for all the fun treats. We wanted to talk to you about Caroline and the hospital. Maybe get more details on the situation there. Can you give us a call back when you have a chance?"

Dad finished the call by saying, "Talk to you soon," and hung up.

Ashton looked at me and said, "It's okay, Lena. She'll call back."

I guess she could see the disappointment on my face. I smiled to let her know I appreciated her for trying to cheer me up.

The rest of the evening dragged on. I finished my homework—still no phone call from Mallory. We ate dinner and did our family devotions with still no phone call from Mallory. We took showers and got ready for bed—still no phone call from Mallory.

Mom and Dad called everyone to my room to say goodnight. Dad sat next to me on the edge of the bed and pulled me in close to him. He whispered, "For tonight, all we can do is pray."

Chapter 2

I tossed and turned most of the night. So many thoughts swirled around in my head. I prayed and I knew we would talk to Mallory soon, but no matter how hard I tried I could not stop my brain from thinking of ways I could help. I could set up a lemonade stand, make bracelets, write letters to my friends and family, and even create a huge sign and attach it to our front door and our car! That way people could learn about Caroline's situation and give money no matter where we were.

When I wasn't thinking of new ideas, I was picturing Caroline's face. I remembered visiting the hospital that day with Mallory. Seeing the kids smile when they saw us made that one of the best days ever. Now I couldn't get Caroline's face out of my head. She probably wasn't smiling anymore. I could not imagine how scared she and her family must be, and I was even more determined that I needed to help them somehow.

As soon as I saw the sun peeking from behind the clouds and through the curtains the next morning, I sat up in my bed. It felt like I hadn't slept at all, though the drool on my pillow told me otherwise.

I wiped my face, jumped out of bed, and hurried down the hall and to my parents' room to tell them my ideas. I lightly tapped on their door and waited for a response.

"Come in." Mom's voice was raspy and low.

I pushed the door open and cautiously took two steps forward.

"Good morning, Lena," Dad said with a big yawn.

I climbed in bed between my parents and started talking.

Mom laid her head back on her pillow, listened, and smiled.

Dad sat up on the edge of the bed. "Lena, this is great and I love your heart. These are some really cool ideas. Hopefully Mallory will call us back after school today, and we can come up with a real plan."

"A *real* plan?" I asked with confusion in my voice. I didn't understand why he said we needed a *real* plan when I had just given him my perfect plan.

"Yes. You can't do all these great ideas at once. And depending on how much Caroline needs, it may not be enough anyway. I am just saying we need to find out all the information before we can decide the best way to help. Okay?"

I know that Dad wasn't trying to make me feel bad, but it really felt like he didn't believe I could help.

"Let's talk about it more after work and school today. There is nothing we can do right now. Tell your sisters it's time to get up and get ready for the day."

Dad flashed a quick smile.

It may not be enough? I thought to myself as I walked toward Amber and Ansley's room. *At least it's something. We have to do something.*

Dad was right about one thing. There was nothing else I could do right now. So I did my best to focus my attention on getting to school on time. When the bus showed up at my house, I was ready.

Morning classes went pretty well, but by lunch I was so glad to be headed to the lunchroom to be with my friends. And it wasn't long before I was laughing until my cheeks hurt, with my best friends Savannah and Emma. They always knew how to make me smile.

We were having so much fun already planning some fun time together that I waited until almost the end of our lunch break to tell them about Caroline. Although they had never met her, they remembered me talking about her. From the expressions on their faces I could tell they felt just as sad as I did.

"You're right, Lena. We have to do something," Savannah said.

"But why do we have to do something?" Joey said as she scooted closer to Emma and across from me—she had been talking to someone else for a few minutes and missed the first part of our conversation. Although I haven't known Joey nearly as long as I have Emma and Savannah, she was really starting to mean just as much to me. She's funny and she cares about friends just as much as I do.

"Well, we were just talking about Caroline's hard time," Emma responded. "She's the little girl Lena met at the children's hospital while she was on tour with Mallory. She's sick and needs our help."

"Apparently all the kids from her hospital may need our help. The hospital is closing," Savannah added.

She was right. I was spending so much time thinking about Caroline that I kept forgetting about the bigger problem. The entire hospital was closing. There had to be more kids than just Caroline that needed our help.

"That's so sad." Joey's entire expression changed. "So, girls, what are we going to do? Can't Mallory help?"

"I'm sure she told me about Caroline so that I would pray for her but I want to do more than that. She is helping as much as she can but they need more than one person to help. Mom and Dad figure they need lots of money."

As soon as I finished that sentence I had a new thought. "That's it! They need a lot money and they need more than one person to help . . . let's have our own fundraiser—a concert!"

Emma cheered, "Yes! Yes! Yes! Let's do it!"

I smiled and cheered with Emma but then quickly looked to see Savannah's response. Savannah doesn't get excited easily and she has a way of thinking things through better than Emma and me. Emma gets excited about everything. She thinks all my fun ideas are good ones which sometimes gets us into a little trouble, like the time we lost track of time while I was filming *Above the Waters*. Savannah didn't think wandering around a strange building when I was supposed to be working was a good idea, but we didn't listen. I guess I didn't want something like that to happen again.

Savannah was smiling but sitting quietly.

"Well, Savannah?" I prodded. "What do you think? Will a concert work?"

Savannah sat up straight. Her eyebrows moved closer together and she leaned forward and started to speak. "I think . . ."

She paused. Joey, Emma, and I focused all of our attention on her. " . . . It's not a bad idea. It could work."

Emma jumped up from the lunch table and began doing her happy dance, which also serves as her hunger dance, birthday dance, and congratulatory dance.

"But . . ." Savannah tried to catch us before we began celebrating too much. "You do know concerts cost money to put on and they require a lot of time to plan, right?"

"Oh, yes! I know that. But I learned so much while I was on tour with Mallory. I know how to plan a good one! And we can ask people to do stuff for free so that it doesn't cost us anything." I was confident. Maybe too confident. But I was positive that together (and with a little adult help too, of course) we could do this!

"Do you think Mallory would perform . . . for free?" Joey asked the obvious question.

"Yup! I am sure of it! I'll talk to my mom and dad as soon as I get home! We are supposed to call Mallory tonight!"

Chapter 3

I couldn't wait to get home. I had my conversation with Mallory all planned out in my head. I knew exactly what I was going to say to her, and I was confident she would not be able to resist my request for her to come to Dallas to perform at our fundraiser for free. I knew she cared about the kids and the hospital as much as I did.

"Mom!" I called out as soon as I burst through the door.

"In here, Lena!" Mom called from the game room. She was sitting on the floor, holding a hot glue gun in the air. All around her were little pieces of colorful fabric. Ashton and Amber were on their knees organizing little buttons.

"What are you doing?" I asked. I wanted to tell her our idea but I couldn't ignore the hot glue gun she was waving at me.

"We are making your sisters' costumes. It's book character day at school this week."

"Ohhhhh!" Now that what they were doing made sense, I was ready to tell her that my friends wanted to help Caroline too.

I told her word-for-word about my conversation with my friends, and she agreed with Savannah. "Oh, yes," she said. "Concerts can raise a lot of money but they are a lot of work! Are you ladies prepared for that kind of commitment?" she asked.

I assured her we were. She told me she was proud of me

for being willing to take on such a huge responsibility and said we could talk about it more over dinner, once Dad was home. I asked if we could call Mallory, and she repeated that we could talk about it more with Dad.

I did my best to keep busy while I waited patiently for Dad. I finished my math and history homework, folded a load of Ashton and Amber's laundry, cleaned my room, and emptied the dishwasher. Finally, I just sat down at the kitchen counter and watched as Mom prepared dinner. I was out of chores to complete, and I was ready to talk to Dad and call Mallory.

Every few minutes I looked at Mom and casually asked, "What time is it?" or "Has Daddy called?" Eventually she suggested that I relax a little bit and stop worrying so much.

"Lena," she said with a firm voice. "Stop worrying. When Dad gets home we will talk."

She was right. Dad arrived home shortly after that. I told him everything I had told Mom and asked if we could call Mallory. I was surprised that he agreed to call Mallory before dinner.

"Should we FaceTime or just call?" he asked.

"Let's just call," I said. Seeing Mallory sometimes made me a little nervous.

Dad picked his phone up and pushed the buttons for her number.

"Hi there, Mallory, it's the Daniels crew!" he said while placing the phone down on the counter and putting it on speaker so Mom and I could hear.

"Hi, Daniels family!" she shouted through the tiny speaker.

"Hi, Mallory!" Mom and I responded.

Mallory asked how everyone was doing and Dad asked her the same. Within a few seconds Dad and Mallory were discussing a few specific questions about the hospital and about Caroline. My heart was beating fast with excitement. I listened carefully just waiting for Dad to finish before I chimed in with the concert idea.

When Dad asked Mallory what exactly we could do to help, she said, "Pray. I sent Lena the information about Caroline because I know how much meeting her impacted her. But I don't want you to feel pressured to help financially. Caroline and the others need a lot of money."

"Oh, I know!" I responded quickly. "I just really want to help. I have been praying and I think I can do more!"

Dad quickly spoke next, "If we wanted to try to help raise money, what are some of our options?"

"Well, Lena, that's great!" Mallory continued. "So . . . the hospital is no longer trying to raise money themselves. They have made the decision to just close. So I am focusing my efforts on helping Caroline and the five other children that will have to go back to their homes in Peru. I would love to raise enough money to keep them here in the United States until they finish their treatments at another hospital. We have already found another one that is willing to provide the services they need but their families need the basics—places to live, food, and clothing."

"How much is that going to be?" I asked.

"Well, for all five families, it's going to be about $150,000."

Mom and Dad looked at each other and shook their

heads. Dad's shoulders drooped some and Mom's eyebrows scrunched together, making her face look worried.

"I still want to help." All the words I had been thinking about all day started to spill out of my mouth. I told Mallory about all my ideas including the sign on our car. She laughed at that one. But when I started to tell her about our idea of having a concert I could hear her quietly saying, "Mmm-hmm."

"So, would you come? Could you come? All of my friends would definitely pay money to meet you!"

She giggled.

As I was talking, more ideas started to pop into my head and I decided to share them all. "We could design T-shirts and sell them like the ones for your tour, except they could have each girl's name on them! So when someone buys a shirt they would know they are helping someone real!"

"I love that idea, Lena!" Mallory sounded really interested.

"And maybe we get people to make and sell things like food or crafts!"

"Wow, Lena, you really have been thinking a lot about this," Dad said, smiling at me. Mom looked surprised by my new ideas too.

"Yes, Lena, I can tell you have! So, if this is something you really want to do, I'll do whatever I can to help!" Mallory added.

I jumped up from the stool I had been sitting on and screamed! Ansley, Ashton, and Amber came running into the room to see what was happening.

"Lena, Lena! What is it?" they questioned.

"We are going to help Caroline and her friends from the children's hospital!" I yelled again.

Austin joined in the fun with a few loud yelps while my mom, dad, and sisters all cheered and celebrated along with Mallory and me!

"Thank you, Mallory! Thank you, Mom and Dad!"

"We're proud of you, Lena." Dad squeezed my shoulders and pulled me close.

"Let's get to work! Because let me tell you, Lena, there is a lot of work to do to make this happen! Let me know as soon as you have a date that will work and where you want to have it!" Mallory said.

"Okay!" I responded and started celebrating with Austin and my sisters all over again, not realizing what I had gotten us all into.

"Lena, one more thing—" Mallory's voice sounded serious again. "Since you are making a commitment now, I think it would be a good idea to call Caroline and tell her your plans."

Dad spoke up, "Are you sure, Mallory? I wouldn't want them to think we can for sure raise the entire amount. We don't know yet how this will all work out."

"Yes, sir, I know you can't make any promises but I think her family would love knowing that there is someone who cares enough to try to help. It would give them a little hope. I can stay on the phone with you if you would like."

Mom and Dad looked at each other and nodded.

I waited for one of them to respond. I wasn't even sure if Caroline would remember me. I had only met her that one time at the hospital. I was sure she had had a ton of visitors since then.

"Okay, let's do that," Dad said.

Mallory asked us to hold on. When she returned to the phone, Caroline and her mother were on the line as well.

"Hi, Lena! It's me, Caroline!"

Hearing her voice made little goose bumps form on my arms, and my eyes immediately filled with tears. They weren't sad tears, I was just so happy to talk to her again.

I took a deep breath and said hello. I introduced her to my family and talked to her mother. I told her that ever since we'd heard the bad news about the hospital closing we had been praying for her and that I really wanted to be able to do something. I could hear sniffles as I talked. I could not tell if they were coming from my family or hers.

Before we ended the call, I told her about my friends and that they were going to work with me to do everything we could.

"So Mom, Dad, my sisters, and my friends Savannah, Emma, and Joey and I promise to work really hard to help." I took a deep breath. "We've just got to do something for you!"

Mallory's voice slipped in. "And we will. Together with God's help, we will do everything we can to help all the families stay here in the US, to get the medical assistance they need."

Caroline's mother continued to thank my family, friends, and me for caring but I wasn't sure why. Caring about Caroline and wanting to help her family was not something I was being asked to do, it was something I was happy to do. Meeting Caroline seemed like a gift to me and it felt like I should be the one saying thank you.

Chapter 4

The next day I told Savannah, Emma, and Joey that we needed to meet during lunch. We all agreed to eat quickly and to use our extra time to find a quiet place where we could talk. I pulled out my black notebook and opened to a blank piece of paper toward the back. I flipped quickly because I didn't want my friends to see my journal entries.

I wrote:

Who: Mallory Winston and Friends Concert
Why: To raise money for Caroline and friends.
Date: ¿
Place: ¿

I looked up at my friends and they each looked at me.

I started, "I talked to Mallory last night. Turns out the hospital does not need the help. They have already decided to close. That's why Caroline needs help, but she is not the only one. There are five kids. They are from Peru and were at the hospital receiving medical treatment for free. The hospital found another place that will get them the treatment they need, but their families need money to pay for living expenses—like a place to live plus food and clothes."

"They don't have hospitals in Peru?" Joey asked.

"I guess they don't have the same kinds of medicines. They need a lot of care," I answered. I told them everything I could remember of what Mallory had told us.

"So what will happen when they finish getting treatment? Will they just go back home then?" Savannah asked.

"Yes. I think so."

"So let's get started." I looked down at the paper and said, "Where do we start?"

"Well, we need to pick a date," Joey answered first.

"But can we pick a date if we don't have a place?" Savannah asked.

"Good point," Emma added. "Let's pick a place first. That way we will have to narrow down dates based on when the place is available."

We looked at each other again. What Emma and Savannah said made sense but it did not help us much.

"Well, we want to do it in Dallas, right? Or do we want to do it in LA?" I asked.

"That would be awesome!" Emma practically screamed.

"Guys," Savannah said calmly. "We would have to spend money to get there and stay there too. How about we do it here and use that money for other things."

Emma blew a little air from the side of her mouth and playfully dropped her head on the table.

Savannah was right, again.

"Maybe at your church?" Joey asked.

I thought for a moment. My church was pretty small, and I wasn't sure enough people could fit. At least not the number of people we needed to help raise close to $150,000.

"Savannah, what about your grandfather's farm?" Emma asked.

"That would be weird and smelly!" Savannah squeaked and I agreed.

After a few moments of unsuccessful suggestions, we decided it was best if each of us went home, talked to our parents, and came back with two places each that we thought would be a good idea.

"Okay, now, let's talk about the fun stuff! The actual concert!" Emma said.

"Well, I talked to Mallory and she agreed to come and perform." Everyone cheered and I continued to speak. "And we can charge extra money if people want to meet her. That happened all the time while I was on tour with her. People would buy a concert ticket but then she would come and hang out with some people before or after the show if they had purchased extra VIP tickets."

"Yes! That's a great idea," Savannah approved.

When I heard her say the word "yes," I reached over and grabbed both of her hands and said, "Thank you!"

We all laughed.

"This is progress, ladies." Joey flashed a bright smile and offered a little encouragement.

I needed it. Somehow we had spent an hour making plans for our big concert but our paper did not look much different than it had when we first started. Joey's words reminded me that this was only the first day.

"Okay, so let's recap quickly before we have to get to class," I said. I looked down at my notes. "Still working on a place, still working on a date, but we have Mallory, and we all like the VIP tickets idea!" Just then I remembered to tell them about my idea for the T-shirts.

I was super-relieved when Savannah smiled and approved again. "I think those are great ideas! I love the idea of buying a shirt with one of the girl's names on it. That's so cool!"

"Can you ask Mallory if she has any celebrity friends that could come too?" Emma looked at me.

"Good idea. I will."

We gathered our things and headed to class. I didn't know how I was going to focus for the rest of the day but I knew I needed to. Ms. Blount was giving us a big test on Friday, and I needed to get a good grade.

When I sat down at my desk I tucked my little black notebook into my backpack and pulled out my large purple binder for history class.

"Let's get started." Ms. Blount's voice was stern as usual but her face seemed to be a little softer. She was almost smiling. "Today is a special day. I want to take a few minutes and talk about people in our community who have made a difference."

I looked at Emma and she looked at me. We both shrugged our shoulders and looked toward Savannah and Joey. They never took their eyes off Ms. Blount and seemed extremely interested in what she was saying.

Ms. Blount turned to the board and we watched quietly as she grabbed a piece of chalk and started to write. Her long flowery dress swayed from left to right with each word and her flat black shoes made a squeaky sound as she inched across the floor. Ms. Blount always wore long dresses and flat shoes. I wondered why, but of course I had never asked her. There were so many things about Ms. Blount that I wondered but never asked. I wondered about her family, and if she had any children. I also wondered whether she had friends. She never ate lunch with the other teachers because she was usually on lunch duty, which meant she spent her lunch break strolling the cafeteria aisles. When she finished writing, she placed her chalk back on the rim of the board, rubbed her hands together, and gently patted them on her sides. Her dress did one final sway as she turned back to face the class. There were four names written on the board.

"Does anyone recognize any of these names?" she asked while her shoes continued to squeak across the floor.

When no one responded, she reached down to her desk and picked up a small stack of colored papers.

"Each piece of paper has a name on it. When you get your paper, find your classmates who have the same color paper. We are going to go to the computer lab to do a little research in small groups."

Ms. Blount handed each of us a piece of paper. Everyone started walking around to find others who had the same name. Ms. Blount encouraged us to move quickly and quietly. This entire activity was a little bizarre but I eagerly welcomed a change in our class routine. Savannah and I both had orange paper. Joey's was green and Emma's was white. We formed little groups and headed to the computer lab quickly and quietly, just like we were told to do.

"Bethany Pickney" was written on my orange sheet of paper. I had no idea who she was but I was ready to find out. We all found empty seats in small groups. When I sat down I typed in Bethany Pickney's name in the search bar and the first thing to pop up on the screen was the face of a little girl. She looked like she was about 10 years old.

I clicked on the picture and my whole group leaned in to start reading. Within the first four sentences we learned that Bethany Pickney raised enough money to open a homeless shelter while she was in college and volunteered for several similar large events around our city.

That's so cool! I thought to myself.

Savannah and I, along with our other group members, wrote down everything we learned about Bethany and looked at several pictures of her as a child and as an adult.

"She's amazing," Savannah said and we all agreed.

Once Ms. Blount noticed that most of the class was finished researching, she asked each group to choose one person to share what we learned. Of course, Savannah volunteered me for the job. I offered it to the others but no one accepted.

I stood up when it was my turn and shared what our group had learned about Bethany and her work with the homeless. The others shared theirs. We learned that Andrew Tate was a pilot, Suzanne Stephens started a school for blind children, and Ashley Wilkinson was the first female surgeon at the hospital where I had been born.

After we each shared, Ms. Blount asked the class, "Did anyone figure out what these people have in common?"

We all looked at each other and waited before speaking. Finally a voice came from the other side of the room. "They all did something to help someone else?"

Ms. Blount nodded. Another voice said, "They all live or lived in Dallas?"

Ms. Blount nodded again and turned to the other side of the room. Her long skirt followed her movements.

"Anyone else?" she asked.

Everyone shook their heads.

Ms. Blount took a deep breath and spoke loudly, "Each of these people made history in our community and each of these people graduated from this middle school."

"No way!" Emma shouted out and immediately threw her hand over her mouth.

Ms. Blount glared at Emma and ignored her outburst. "At one time they sat right where you are sitting and they could have been you. Remember that what you are doing today not only matters today but it matters in the future." Ms. Blount had managed to capture the entire class's attention.

She continued to talk. "Over the next week we are going to study the impact these individuals have had in detail. But today I want you to think about the fact that one day you too could have a major impact on our community."

Ms. Blount walked toward the door and told us to follow her back to class. As we walked, the class was not as quiet as it had been. I could hear people talking about Bethany Pinkney, as well as the others we had just learned about.

As I listened, a new idea came to my mind and the moment the bell rang I blurted it out to Savannah, Emma, and Joey.

"Here! We have to have our concert here at our school!"

Although their initial response was "no way," it did not take long to convince them that our school would be the best place to have the concert. And later in the evening when I told Mom and Dad, they thought it was a great idea too!

Once I had everyone on board, I needed to figure out a

way to convince our school. That evening before bed, Mom and I talked about what I should do next. She suggested I schedule a meeting with the principal. That sounded scary and I yelled, "No way!" Then I begged her to come up with an easier idea.

I didn't know the principal but he seemed to only like the 8th graders. Every day he walked right past the 6th grade lunch tables and stood near the older kids. He didn't say much but he smiled at them before making his announcements. He never smiled at us. Mom said it was because they have known him longer and have learned that he's not mean. I asked if she could do it without me. Of course, she did not agree to that but she said that if I set the meeting up, she would go with me.

"I don't know how to set a meeting up!"

"Sure you do," Mom assured me. "You can either go to his office and speak with the front desk staff or you can write an email and I'll send it."

She grabbed both of my hands in hers as I laid in my bed, looked at me, and saw the fear in my eyes. "Lena," she said. "God has helped you through so many other things. Who gave you the courage to be in a movie?"

"God did," I answered.

"And who gave you the courage to stand up on stage and share your story with thousands of people?"

I smiled and started nodding my head. "God did!"

"So, I am pretty sure He will help you talk to your principal. Just ask Him. And remember this, Lena. This is something you and your friends really want to do. So you need to take charge."

She squeezed my hands tight and let go.

Mom was right. Over the last year I had definitely learned that there was no reason to be afraid. All I needed to do was ask God for help.

Mom grabbed a piece of paper from my nightstand and wrote:

2 Timothy 1:7—For God has not given us a spirit of fearfulness, but one of power, love, and sound judgment.

After writing, she looked at me and said, "Lena, you have been so determined to help Caroline ever since you met her! Do not let a little fear and nervousness stop you now! Pray this tonight. When you are ready, let me know how you want to set up the meeting." She handed me the paper, kissed me on my forehead, and walked out.

A few minutes later Ansley danced her way through our bedroom door with Austin prancing behind her. They both bounced into her bed. After burying herself under her new purple comforter she peeked over to see if I was still awake.

"You missed Dad's story! It's a new book he got about two sisters and it's really good!" she said.

"I know. I just needed to talk to Mom a little," I replied.

"About what? Caroline?" Ansley sat up a little. She looked extremely inquisitive and ready to talk.

I welcomed the conversation. Mom's words, the Scripture she gave me to pray, and Caroline's face were racing around in my head, and talking seemed to help me process things better.

"Yeah, so I have to ask the principal of my school if we can have a fundraising concert there," I said. Ansley's eyes popped open wide. "I know, right? So do you think I should email him, write a note and leave it in the office for him, or go into the office and ask if I can have an appointment?"

Ansley gasped. "Write a note," she said and paused for a second. I could tell she was still thinking. "Draw a smiley face on it too."

Ansley giggled and flopped back onto her pillow. Austin snuggled next to her and she quietly said, "Good night, Lena."

I reached over and turned off my lamp. "Night."

Chapter 5

As usual, the next morning I was up before my sisters. I grabbed the little paper Mom had left on my nightstand and crept down the hall toward the game room. I was expecting to see my dad sitting in his favorite big brown chair but he wasn't there. The room was dark and empty. I was a little sad. I loved spending alone time with Dad in the mornings. I could ask him questions and get his advice on problems I was having. I could also talk to him about God and the Bible. But this morning I did not really need any advice. I already knew just what I needed to do.

I pulled a sheet of paper from the stack next to the printer and picked up a chewed-up pencil from the middle of the floor. "Austin!" I said to myself and giggled. Austin loved eating anything we left on the floor, especially crayons and pencils. I checked to make sure there was still enough lead left for me to write with and there was. I just couldn't make any mistakes because there was no eraser left.

I looked down at the paper and took a deep breath. I unfolded Mom's paper with 2 Timothy 1:7 written on it and laid it on top. I closed my eyes and said to myself, "Dear God, help me to be courageous."

I immediately opened my eyes and started writing.

Dear Mr. Fraser,

My name is Lena Daniels. I know you don't know

*me but I am one of the 6th grade students at your
school. I have a big favor that I would like to ask
you. There are a few sick children that I think
we can help. They are from Peru but they live in
Nashville, TN right now. The children's hospital
where they have been staying is closing. They
cannot go home because their hospitals do not have
the kind of medicine they need. I know that we can
help them. I know that our school can help them.
Can I meet with you and share my ideas, please?
They need our help.*

I signed my name at the bottom and included my mother's telephone number.

I folded the paper nicely and placed it an envelope. I wrote "To Mr. Fraser" across the front and smiled.

I couldn't wait to show Mom and Dad!

I sat quietly until I heard a few sounds coming from the kitchen. "Mom?" I whispered as loudly as I could.

Dad poked his head into the room and said, "Hey, babe. How long have you been up?"

Before I could answer I was greeted by a few wet kisses from Austin. He placed his two front paws directly onto my envelope and then stretched out on his back. "Hey, boy!" I said while shooing him over just a little. Dad immediately gave in to Austin's big brown eyes and wide-open belly. I laughed as he squatted down and gave Austin his morning rub. I slipped the wrinkled envelope from under him and tucked it into the pocket of my long blue robe.

Dad was so occupied with Austin that he didn't even

notice. I decided I would wait and tell him and Mom about it at the same time.

"Okay, that's enough, boy!" Dad said while hopping up onto his feet.

"Want some coffee?" Dad pretended to ask with a serious face before leaving the room.

"Daddy! You know I can't drink coffee!"

I could still hear him laughing at his own joke as he shuffled a few mugs around in the kitchen.

By the time I made my way into the kitchen Ansley and Ashton were waddling their way in as well.

"What's for breakfast, Daddy?" Ansley asked.

"Can I have waffles?" Ashton begged.

"Eggs," Dad responded to them both while digging for the large black pan he liked to use.

"Lena, go tell Amber that it is time to get up."

I did as I was told and came back a few moments later with a weepy Amber just a few steps behind me. We were used to hearing Amber crying for a few minutes in the morning until she became fully awake.

"It's okay, Amber," I tried to comfort her. "I know you don't like getting up, but sometimes we all have to do things we don't like doing."

I don't know if my words helped or not but in about three minutes Amber was smiling.

We ate our breakfast, got dressed, packed our lunches, and headed off to school for the day.

It wasn't until lunch that I remembered I'd left my letter for Mr. Fraser in the pocket of my blue robe. When I told Savannah, Emma, and Joey what I had written, Emma looked at me and asked, "Why not just talk to him?"

I gasped. "No way!"

"I understand that the letter is easier but talking to him is faster." Emma tried to persuade me.

"He's right there," Joey added.

"Let's just go do it together. We are a team, right?" Emma said, while standing up.

"And he's right there," Joey said again and stood next to Emma. I looked up at them both and dropped my head.

"Okay," I mumbled while jumping to my feet.

Savannah did not move.

"Savannah," I said in my firmest voice.

She crossed her arms and casually shook her head.

Mr. Fraser walked right past us as he headed toward the side of the room where the 8th graders sat.

"We have to do it now," Emma said right before she called, "Mr. Fraser!"

I couldn't believe my ears. I gulped and froze with my back still facing him.

Mr. Fraser took two steps back and turned in our direction. "Yes? Good afternoon."

Savannah's cheeks turned red, and she slowly stood up.

I turned and quickly said, "Good afternoon," while focusing my attention on his brown square-toed shoes. I liked the way his shoelaces seemed to play peek-a-boo with his navy pants. When I heard Savannah's voice again I looked up quickly and made eye contact with Mr. Fraser for the first time ever.

"This is Lena Daniels," she said. Mr. Fraser's face was

the color of caramel and I could see a few pieces of prickly hair on his head, but he was basically bald. His cheeks were round and they made his face look soft and happy.

"Hi there, Lena Daniels. I know a lot about you." His smile was wide so I stretched my lips as wide as I could and smiled back.

"Well, sir," I started. "My friends and I were talking and we have an idea. Do you think we could have a meeting with you?"

Mr. Fraser's smile closed just a little and he seemed to lean back on the heels of his nice brown shoes. I could now see all of his shoelaces.

"Well, of course," he said. "We can go to my office now or we can just meet right here for a few moments if you'd like." He pulled his hands out of his pockets, clasped them together, and stretched forward in my direction.

"Now's good, sir!" Emma responded quickly.

Both she and Mr. Fraser looked right at me.

I took a deep breath and started from the beginning. As I talked I occasionally glanced down at his shoelaces to see what they were doing. When I saw them peek out I could continue with my thoughts and when they disappeared I would quickly move ahead in my ideas and plans.

I finished with, "Can our school help? I have to do something."

Mr. Fraser was smiling. "Well now, Ms. Lena Daniels and friends." He looked at each of us and nodded. "I agree."

I let out a long quiet breath when I heard his words.

He continued, "We do have to do something."

"Yay!" Joey cheered a little.

"I think you girls have a great idea but planning events like you have in mind is hard . . ."

"Work." Emma finished his sentence and giggled.

"We know. But I know how to work hard, and I know we can do it. So can we do it here? Can our concert be here at the school? Please?" I asked.

Mr. Fraser bit his bottom lip, smiled, and said, "Yes. I think so. I have a staff meeting this afternoon. I will talk to my team and see what we can do."

Mr. Fraser shook each of our hands, including Savannah's, and left.

As soon as he turned to walk away Emma, Joey, Savannah, and I collapsed in our chairs and started to giggle uncontrollably until we heard Ms. Blount announce that we only had 10 minutes left before our next class.

"We better get going, guys!" Savannah encouraged us.

By the end of the day my cheeks were hurting from smiling so much. I tried to remind myself that Mr. Fraser had not officially agreed yet, but something in my heart knew that he would.

When I told Mom, Dad, and my sisters the news we all cheered and shouted. I was sure to tell them that he had not actually agreed yet but that I was almost certain he would.

"This calls for a celebration!" Dad insisted.

"How about donuts for breakfast tomorrow?" Ansley suggested, and we all cheered again.

Chapter 6

The next morning Dad kept his word. We woke to a lovely box of chocolate covered and glazed donuts waiting on the kitchen counter. Since I take the school bus Dad wanted to make sure I could still enjoy my favorite breakfast before I left.

By the time I got to school I was so full of sugar and excitement that I could barely sit still. Thankfully, Ms. Blount did not wait until the end of the day to hand me a white envelope with my full name written across the front.

"Thank you," I said and she smiled just enough to let me know there was good news inside the envelope.

I reached down and slid it into my black notebook. I heard Savannah, Emma, and Joey giggle softly next to me.

During our first break between classes, we found a quiet corner at the end of the long yellow hall and ripped the letter open.

My eyes scanned the paper quickly before reading each word aloud to my friends.

Dear Lena Daniels and Team,

Thank you for taking the time to tell me about your recent visit to the children's hospital and about your friend from Peru. I was really touched by you and your friends' hearts and your ideas to raise the needed funds. We would love for our school to be

*a part of something so amazing. We have asked
Ms. Blount to work with you on this event. She
will help you choose a date and coordinate with
our staff and any vendors you may need. With her
supervision and guidance, I know you will do an
amazing job! Ms. Blount is eager to help and ready
to set the plan in motion when you are.*

Thank you for inviting our school to be a part of this.
Sincerely,

Mr. Fraser

Emma, Savannah, and Joey cheered and chuckled after
every sentence. But Emma could not help but whimper a
little when she heard Ms. Blount's name.

"This is going to be FANTASTIC!" I shouted and
bounced up and down a few times.

"But Ms. Blount?" I could tell from Emma's face that
she was trying to focus on the bright side but she couldn't
resist vocalizing her concern.

I had to admit that I understood her hesitation. Ms.
Blount was not known for being friendly and helpful to
the students. I reminded Emma of the beautiful gift she'd
helped them make when I filmed the movie, and that Ms.
Blount was the reason having it at the school had even
popped into my head.

Emma smiled and I could see that she was starting to
soften up to the idea.

She let out a full smile when Savannah reread the
words, "Ms. Blount is eager to help . . . !"

The bell rang and we scattered to our next class.

Before pulling out my math book, I pulled out my black notebook and opened to the back pages with our meeting notes and ideas. I filled the empty space next to the word "place" with the word "school." Then I placed the ripped envelope with Mr. Fraser's letter in it on top of the page and closed the book.

When I heard my teacher begin to talk, I immediately pulled my math book out and opened it. I tried to focus, but the more numbers I heard the more my brain drifted with thoughts of Caroline, Mallory, and T-shirt designs. So I gently slid my notebook from underneath my math book and laid it open on top and started drawing.

I drew the best T-shirt I could and wrote Caroline's name in bubble letters. Right next to that I drew another one, but this time instead of bubble letters, I drew swirling lines all around the name. I repeated this same thing, replacing the swirls with flowers, hearts, and stars, until I had a page covered in T-shirt designs.

I had drifted so far into my own thoughts that I did not hear my math teacher call my name until I felt his hand on the back of my chair.

"Lena?" He spoke in a firm voice. "What do you have there? Hand it to me, please."

He held his hand out. "But . . ." I winced.

He stood still, with his hand stretched out even further, and I had no choice but to give him my black notebook.

I was petrified. Not only was I going to be in big trouble with Mom and Dad, but what would Mr. Fraser and Ms. Blount think? Everyone would be so disappointed in me.

As I sat through the rest of class I tried to hold back the tears. "God, please don't let him tell anyone," I thought to myself over and over again.

After class I slowly gathered my things, hoping that he would remember to hand my book back. Savannah, Emma, and Joey headed for the door. They turned and waved for me to join them.

"Sorry, Lena," Savannah said while Joey patted me on the back.

"Uhmmmm, Lena?" Emma said wearily. "Isn't that the same book you journal in?"

"OH NO!" I cried out. I stopped walking and finally let the tears fall freely. This was even worse than I had originally thought.

This was the same notebook I took with me to LA while I was filming the movie and on tour. This was the same book I talked to God in. I had told God some pretty personal things, and thinking about my teachers or anyone else reading it made my stomach and head hurt. Not only was I going to be in big trouble, but now I was mortified.

My friends wrapped their arms around me and squeezed.

"It will be okay, Lena, I promise," Emma encouraged.

"Yeah, it will be," Joey and Savannah added.

They walked me to the cafeteria and we took our seats at our normal table.

Emma tried to make me smile. I appreciated her for trying even though she knew it wouldn't work. I watched quietly as they ate. The knots in my stomach were taking up so much space in my stomach that there was no room for food.

"Here he comes," Joey whispered from across the table.

I knew who it was because I saw his shoelaces before I even heard his voice.

"Lena? Can you come to my office?" Mr. Fraser stood over me.

I stood up slowly and asked, "Now?"

"Yes." He turned and headed toward the doors. With my head down, I followed him.

As soon as I stepped into Mr. Fraser's office I spotted my black notebook laying on his desk.

Before he shut the door, Ms. Blount joined us.

"Lena," she started.

"I am so sorry," I started before either Mr. Fraser or Ms. Blount could say anything else. "I was just so excited by the news that I couldn't, well, I mean I was trying, I was just having a really hard time . . ."

"Lena, let me speak," Ms. Blount interrupted. "When Mr. Fraser told us about the idea of a fundraiser here at school I was excited to hear that one of our students wanted to take on a task so big. But I was hesitant to agree to help because it is such a huge responsibility."

I looked down.

"But then he told us who the students were that wanted to lead it, and I knew I had to help. Lena, you are one of the most responsible students I know, and your friends too. I love teaching you, and I always know I can count on you to do the right thing."

As she talked I looked up. I wanted to smile, but it still felt like I was in trouble. So I held it in.

"I know what happened in math class today and I am sure it was a mistake. Right?"

I nodded.

"We want you to know that working on this event is great, and we are very proud of you, but you have to remember to respect your teachers and the other people around you. Do you understand what I am trying to say?"

I looked away and thought for a few seconds. I wasn't sure. I knew that I should not have been drawing T-shirt designs during math class, but I didn't think I was being disrespectful to my teacher. I was just excited by the news that our school would help and I wanted to get things moving.

Mr. Fraser took a few steps toward me and said, "As we move forward with helping you to plan this event, we want you to remember that your teachers and your school-work are just as important as helping your friends from Peru. It's not fair to them if you are distracted. We know the doodling in math was a mistake but we want to make sure you understand the importance of what we are saying. Tomorrow you may want to offer an apology to your teacher before math class begins."

"Yes, sir," I said quietly. I knew I had made a mistake and I was grateful that I was not in more trouble than this. I was more than willing to say I was sorry.

Mr. Fraser reached over to his desk and handed me my black notebook. I didn't know if he or Ms. Blount had read any of it but there was nothing I could do about that. I was just happy to have it back.

I clutched my notebook close to my chest with both hands. "Thank you!" I said with a little excitement.

Mr. Fraser smiled and turned toward Ms. Blount. She

was standing straight, with her arms crossed in front of her chest.

"Ok. Now, since you are both here, you should set a time for your first group planning meeting."

As Ms. Blount let her arms fall by her waist my stomach formed little knots. The thought of meeting with her alone frightened me.

"I think my mom and dad would like to meet too," I spoke up in a hurry before she could suggest a time.

"Okay, I will email them to see when they are available. You can talk to the rest of your team—Savannah, Emma, and Joey—and see when a good time might be for them as well."

"Okay."

"Then we will officially schedule it." Ms. Blount spoke her last words directly to Mr. Fraser.

He looked at her and then at me and smiled. "Sounds like a good plan to me!"

He patted me on the shoulder and dismissed me. "Back to class, Lena."

"Okay, thank you," I said and headed out of his office and down the hall. Lunch was over and it was time to join my friends in Ms. Blount's class for the rest of the afternoon. As soon as I saw them I flashed a quick smile to let them know everything was going to be fine.

Emma playfully wiped her hand across her forehead and let out a sigh of relief. Savannah, Joey, and I just chuckled quietly.

Ms. Blount stood at the front of the room and said, "Okay, class, it's time to get focused. Let's get started."

Although she was looking straight ahead it felt like she was speaking directly to me. I took my black notebook, placed it in my backpack, and zipped it closed. I was determined to show Ms. Blount and Mr. Fraser that focusing on my classwork would not be a problem.

Chapter 7

By the time I finished my last class I was bursting with joy. Emma, Joey, and I spent the bus ride home drawing new shirts and coming up with a few event titles. Emma liked "The Biggest Giver Event" and Joey loved the simple "The Big Event."

I knew choosing a title for this was going to be hard so we decided it was best to ask Savannah for ideas too. Something she came up with might be a better one. We all agreed that having her come up with a new one was the best idea of them all.

I bounced off the bus and ran toward the house. "Mom?" I called out as soon as I burst through the door.

I didn't hear Mom but I was greeted by a warm wet tongue as it swiped across my knees.

"Austin!" I dropped my bags and reached down to play with him. Just a few seconds later, Ashton and Amber joined Austin and me on the floor.

"Where's Mom?" I asked my sisters.

"She's helping Ansley with her science homework," Amber said while rustling the hair on Austin's head.

I jumped up and ran to find Mom.

"Mom? Mom? Mom!" I called.

Mom was sitting on the floor facing Ansley, with a stack of flashcards in her lap.

"Mom!"

"Oh, hi, Lena! How was your day?" Mom turned toward me while raising a new card for Ansley.

"It was great! Mr. Fraser said yes! And Ms. Blount will be helping us."

"Oh, wow! That's great, Lena. I can't wait to hear more once Ansley and I are done."

Ansley smiled at me and turned back to face Mom. Studying was serious business around here sometimes.

I continued to talk. I spoke a little louder this time to make sure Mom knew how exciting my news was . . . certainly more exciting and way more important than Ansley's science. "Ms. Blount said she is going to email you so we can all meet. And I created new . . ."

Mom interrupted me. "Lena, that's really great. I can't wait to hear more in a little bit. Let me finish helping Ansley now." She turned her attention back toward Ansley.

I stepped a little closer to them both. I just couldn't wait to tell Mom everything. "But, Mom! Emma, Joey, and I . . ."

Mom put the flashcard down and looked at me. Her face was very serious, and I knew immediately that she was not happy with my interruptions. "Lena. I am sorry, but you are going to have to wait. Don't you think you are being a little rude to your sister? Her science test is just as important as your news. I want to talk to you both, but you will have to wait your turn." Mom's voice was stern.

I quietly turned and walked out of the room toward my bedroom. Amber and Ashton followed me.

"Lena, so Ms. Blount is going to help you?" Ashton asked.

I nodded.

"But Lena, aren't you scared of her?" Amber joined the conversation.

"No, not really. Well, not that much anymore." I hurried an answer out before asking them to give me a little time alone. I was feeling a little sad that Mom didn't want to hear about my plans.

No one cares, I thought to myself, as I stretched my body across my bed and smashed my face against my pillow. There were so many exciting things to share, decisions to be made, and planning to do, but no one other than my friends and I seemed to really care. The more I thought about it the more frustrated I felt.

First, I have to wait all day to do any actual work on the fundraiser, and now I have to wait even longer.

"Lena?" Dad's voice interrupted my thoughts.

I raised my head slowly. "Hi, Daddy."

"What's going on? Mom said you had some exciting news and needed to talk." Dad looked confused.

I took a deep breath, pulled myself up from the pillow, and told Dad everything. Well, everything except for the conversation with Mr. Fraser and Ms. Blount in the office. I knew I needed to but I wanted to get all the good news out first.

When I finished, Dad said, "Wow, Lena. This all sounds really great! You have a location and more help! I'll talk to Mom about the meeting with Ms. Blount. And we need to go ahead and set a date with Mallory now that you actually have a place for this big event!"

Dad's enthusiasm was contagious but I could feel my smile starting to fade. "Daddy, there's more," I said with less excitement. Then I told him about my doodles and what Ms. Blount and Mr. Fraser had said.

"Is this why you were sad when I walked in?" he asked.

"No. Well, sort of." I paused and thought for a second. "I was just really excited to tell Mom everything."

Dad sat quietly and listened.

"But she was helping Ansley." I finished talking and I knew I needed to apologize. I had done exactly what Mr. Fraser and Ms. Blount had talked to me about at school. I needed to remember to respect others even though I was really excited about my own plans and ideas. *This is going to be hard work in more ways than one.*

"I'll tell Ansley and Mom that I am sorry."

"I think that would be the right thing to do. I'm sure they will appreciate it, and everyone will love to see your T-shirt designs and hear your news!" Dad grinned and told me to come out to the kitchen with everyone else.

I followed him and joined my family around the kitchen table. Ansley was finished studying and was busy coloring in her new coloring book, and Ashton and Amber were playing a game of tic-tac-toe. Mom was standing in front of the open refrigerator door trying to decide what we should eat for dinner.

"Want to color?" Ashton asked.

"Maybe later," I answered. I reached down and pulled out my black notebook. "Do you guys want to see the shirts I am designing for the fundraiser?"

"Oh, yes!" Mom closed the refrigerator door and joined us at the table. Amber and Ashton sat up on their knees

and leaned in close. I opened the notebook and everyone immediately started choosing their favorite ones.

"Lena, can we show Mallory?" Ansley squealed.

"Oh, yes! What a great idea. I'll call her." Mom grabbed her phone and dialed.

When Mallory's face appeared on the screen we all giggled and moved so close together that I could feel pieces of Amber's hair brushing against my cheeks.

"Hi, Daniels family!" Mallory's smile was big as always.

"Hi!" we all shouted back at her.

"Girls." Mom looked at us and said, "Everybody back up a little so that Mallory can see everyone." Mom pointed out that only pieces of each of our faces were actually visible on the tiny screen.

"Hi, Mallory," Dad joined the conversation. "Lena has been doing some planning and working on some details for the fundraiser, and it looks like this event is actually happening!"

"Wow! Lena, that's great news! So, you have a place?"

"Yes! My school has agreed to let us have it there! Now we just need to choose a date."

"I'll get Sammy, my road manager, to email you some options that work with my calendar. This is so awesome. I can't wait to share the news with Caroline and the others!"

"Great. We are going to schedule a meeting with the school staff that is helping and any other adults that may want to pitch in for early next week. Having your available dates will be helpful," Dad said.

"Okay, sounds good. So I'll perform and then what else

do you have planned? Also, have you thought about how much you will sell tickets for? Details like that?"

"Oh, no, not yet." I kept listening but added "ticket price" to my to-do list in my notebook. I also needed to remember the extra cost of VIP tickets if Mallory was okay with doing that at the concert too.

"Okay, well you will need to create a budget so that you know how much the event will cost you. This will help you decide how much to sell the tickets for and give you an idea of how much you will make."

I looked at Mom and Dad. They were both nodding their heads like they knew exactly what Mallory was talking about, but I had no idea what she meant. No one else had mentioned a budget or cost. Actually, I didn't even know what would cost money. The point was to raise money not to spend it. Mallory had already agreed to come for free and I was pretty sure I wasn't going to have to pay the school either. *What will cost money?*

I decided to talk to Mom and Dad about it later. For now I just added the word "budget" to my to-do list and filled Mallory in on our ideas for the T-shirts.

"I love that, Lena!" She clapped her hands together when I mentioned the shirts with each patient's name. "Do you know anyone that can print the shirts? Maybe we can get them donated."

"Donated?" I asked.

"Yeah, companies will sometimes donate things when they know you are doing something for a good cause. Otherwise you will have to spend a lot of money up front on buying those and getting them printed. You should try to get bottles of water donated too."

I was trying to make a note of everything Mallory was saying. My to-do list now covered an entire page.

"Check with your school. They may have a good printer for the flyers and other advertisements like posters and a vendor for the shirts. Let me know what they say."

I looked to Mom and Dad for help. I had not thought of any of the things Mallory was saying and the more she talked the more overwhelmed I felt. Before this conversation I felt like I had already accomplished so much. Now I began to wonder if I was getting in over my head.

"Well, Mallory, looks like you've given Lena quite a long list of marching orders! We'll sort it all out and have some more details for you after the weekend and our meeting next week," Dad said.

"Perfect!" Mallory said in a chipper voice. "I'm going to call the families now and tell them the plan! They will be so excited to know someone is trying to help!"

"Sounds good. Thanks, Mallory!" Mom leaned over our heads to make sure Mallory could see her face.

"Bye, girls!"

"Bye!" we all said at the same time.

Once Mom pushed the end button on her phone I cried, "WHAT?!"

Mom and Dad laughed but I was serious. Suddenly this all felt like a really bad idea.

"This is way too much work!" I cried.

"Oh, Lena, this is why you have a team. Dad and I will help you—Ms. Blount, Mallory, Emma, Savannah, and

Joey—we are in this together. And we are sure others will step forward to help as word of this great cause spreads in the community."

"And don't forget—God will help you too. Just ask Him," Dad added before telling us to put on our shoes.

He looked at Mom and asked, "Should we just get a pizza?"

Mom nodded and we all scurried off to our rooms to get ready before heading out for dinner.

When we finally made it back home, I was exhausted. This day had been packed with so many new ideas, questions, and things to think about. I dragged myself straight to bed.

Right before I closed my eyes I spotted the little paper Mom had given me. I reached for it and looked around to make sure Ansley was still in the bathroom before praying out loud.

Dear God,

I am starting to feel like this event was not a good idea. There is just so much to do. I really want to help Caroline and the other families, but I don't know as much as I thought I did. Thanks for giving me friends and people that want to help with this event, but I think I will need more than that. Will you help me too, please?

Oh, and will you help me to not get into any more trouble at school or at home?

Ansley waltzed into the room before I could say amen, so I just moved my lips and said it without making a sound.

"Ansley?" I whispered.

"Yes, Lena?"

"I am sorry for being rude when you were trying to study for science. I hope you pass your test," I said.

Ansley yawned out the words, "It's okay. Goodnight, Lena."

"Goodnight, Ansley," I yawned out too.

Chapter 8

The next morning I woke up excited for the weekend. It was only Friday but that meant that once I made it through the school day, I would have all weekend to work on my to-do list.

As usual, my friends and I gathered around the lunch table to work as we ate. As we scrolled down the page, words like "donations," "budget," and "vendors" caused Emma's eyes to bulge out and Joey to gasp loudly while Savannah searched for words to try to help everyone stay calm.

In the short time we had for lunch, all we managed to do was make a list of more questions and more tasks that needed to be done. It wasn't hard to see that we were going to need to meet more often than a few lunchbreaks. I proposed a Saturday early morning time to meet extra but Savannah was a little hesitant to agree. There were so many other activities we were involved in. She reminded us that it was almost time for track season, which meant a Friday evening track practice. She also had church choir rehearsal, and we each had a few other family commitments.

"It's going to be impossible to get everything done," she said, not sounding very optimistic.

"Yeah, we just don't have enough time. We still have homework, projects, and chores to take care of," Joey agreed while adding more reasons why this event seemed to be falling apart before it even really started.

I sank down in my chair and watched as each of my friends' faces started to take on more and more defeat. I could tell they were no longer feeling excited, and I needed to find a way to keep them involved and enthusiastic.

I mustered some energy and said, "Guys, yes, it's a lot of work but we can do it. We are a team. Remember, this is not about us. We are doing this for other kids that need our help. God will help us."

No one smiled. I looked down at the growing to-do list and back up at my friends. I remembered what Dad had told me about reading the Bible and knew I needed to tell my friends.

"Guys, remember the devotionals I gave you?"

They nodded.

"Well, my dad gave me one first because I had told him I really wanted to read the Bible but it just seemed like too much information and it was overwhelming."

Emma, Savannah, and Joey stared at me intently. They also looked confused.

"So, Dad told me that you read the Bible the same way you eat an elephant."

I couldn't say those words without laughing. They joined me.

"Lena, what are you talking about?" Emma blurted out in between giggles.

"Well, you would eat it one bite at a time, right? Just like you do anything else. So no matter how big it is, you have to take it in little pieces."

I watched as Dad's words started to make sense to them too. I reached down and picked up the black notebook. "Guys, let's eat this elephant!"

"Yeah!" Emma was the first to cheer and everyone else joined in.

"We can't do all of this in one day, but let's just choose one thing on the list that we can do today."

Everyone agreed. We each scanned the list. My eyes stopped at the words "event title."

"Guys, let's name our big day!"

Emma and Joey shared their ideas with Savannah. Savannah listened and sat quietly for a second before saying, "The Big Give."

Emma closed her eyes and smiled. "Ooooh, I like it."

"Me too," Joey said.

"Perfect! It's a combination of both of your ideas! Let's check it off the list!"

I drew a big checkmark next to "event title" and filled in the name of our event—THE BIG GIVE.

"That felt good!" Savannah flashed a huge smile.

It did feel good and I was glad to see my friends smiling again. We decided that was enough planning for the day. We each agreed to talk to our parents about starting our proposed Saturday meetings next weekend, after we had a chance to meet with Ms. Blount and a concert date had been selected.

As we headed back to class, I listened to Savannah and Emma talk about the upcoming track practices. "They start today," Savannah said casually.

"It's only if you want to start working out before actual tryouts."

"Wait! What? I didn't know that they started today!" I admitted.

"Oh," Savannah spoke more cautiously. "Lena, I am

sorry. It's only for people that were on the volleyball team. Since we don't have any more games, coach said he would start training us for track. Sorry."

They all stopped smiling and watched for my reaction. I wasn't mad at my friends for not telling me, but I was sad that I didn't know and couldn't go. It was bad enough that I missed playing volleyball over the summer and on the school team because of the movie and tour. Now that I was back, I had worked really hard to rejoin my normal life. Yet somehow, listening to them talk reminded me that I was still missing so much.

"Sorry, Lena," Joey said again.

Emma could tell from my facial expression that I was sad so she tried to comfort me. "Maybe we could ask if they will make a special exception since you weren't here for most of the volleyball season?" she said while wrapping her arms around my shoulders. "Or we can just show you everything we learn on Saturday after our meeting! Don't worry, we won't let you miss anything important!"

My friends' concern and willingness to cheer me up made me smile. I rested my head on Emma's shoulder, and we all made our way down the crowded halls and into class.

I tried not to think about how much fun they were all going to have together every Friday without me, and I did a pretty good job until the end of the day came. It was time for the bus ride home and I knew that I would be alone. I knew a few other people on the bus by now, but I always sat next to Joey and Emma so I never really talked to anyone else.

I sat next to the first familiar face I saw. Her name was Bri, and we talked for most of the ride. She asked if I was the girl in the movie, and I told her yes. I was grateful that she didn't ask for my autograph and she didn't even act weird once she knew. I also told her about The Big Give event that my friends and I were planning and she got really excited.

When I mentioned that Mallory Winston was going to be performing she raised both hands to her cheeks and let out a squeaky scream. This made me laugh. I pulled out the picture of Caroline that Mallory had sent, and I told my new friend all about her, her family, and the other families we were going to help. Bri listened carefully and said she could not wait to buy a T-shirt.

The bus pulled up to the front of my house, and I told her I would give her more information soon. "And thanks for being so excited, because having fun while helping others was our goal!"

She smiled and waved as I jumped off the bus. As I walked to my door I told myself that I needed to talk to new people more often. I love my best friends but there was something fun about meeting new people.

Over dinner that evening, I told Mom and Dad about Bri and that even though I was sad to miss the early track practices, I was grateful to meet a new friend.

Dad laughed because he remembered how meeting new people used to scare me. While we sat around the dinner table Dad told me he was proud of me. "It's so good to see my Lena grow and mature in every way. You have come so far since this whole adventure with Mallory and the movie began."

I smiled shyly and Mom patted my hand across the table and sent a grin to Dad. "That's our girl."

After a few quiet moments and last bites of dinner, Dad sent Ansley for his Bible and said he had a Scripture he wanted to share with us.

We all watched as Ansley's two curly ponytails bounced down the hall and back again with Dad's big black Bible. Ansley handed it to Dad and then crawled up on his lap. Dad pushed his chair back a little from the table so that she could fit.

"Okay, girls, listening to Lena's story about her new friend on the bus reminds me of Matthew 7:12 which says, 'Therefore, whatever you want others to do for you, do also the same for them.'"

Dad looked at each of us. "Do you know what this means?"

Amber was the first to answer. "Be nice!"

Dad nodded his head. "That's right. If you like it when people are nice to you, be nice back! And if you like it when someone tries to make you feel better when you are sad or lonely, do that when you see someone else who is sad or lonely!"

"Yeah, I like it when people make me laugh. So I always try to make other people laugh," Ansley added.

"That's right, girls. God always wants us to treat others how we want to be treated. So be kind, be patient, be forgiving, and always care about the people around you. Like Lena's friend on the bus today. She could have been mean to Lena or ignored her, but she wasn't. She talked to her and was very nice." Dad leaned back in his chair and gave Ansley a squeeze.

Mom sat forward and rested both arms on the table. "This is also why our family is going to work really hard to help Caroline and the other families. If something were to happen to you guys we would want and need people to help us too. Right?"

"Right!"

Mom stretched her arms out, grabbed Amber and Ashton's hands, and said, "Let's pray. Ansley, you want to?"

Ansley popped up from Dad's chest and started, "Dear God, thank you for our family. Thank you for teaching us how to treat each other and the people around us. Will you help us not to be selfish but to always treat others how we like to be treated? Will you help Caroline and help us to raise a lot of money for her? In Jesus' name, amen!"

"Amen!"

"Alright, girls, clear the table," Dad said as he got up. Mom joined him.

"Oh, Lena, we talked to Ms. Blount today. She can't meet until next Thursday. She said she wanted you to be able to give Mallory a date as soon as possible so we just went ahead and chose one!"

"Wait? You did? When, Mommy? When?" I begged to know.

"May 2nd!"

"Dad and I already talked to Sammy, and Mallory has it on her calendar! It's on the school calendar too. So, we are all set!"

I ran to Mom and jumped onto my tippy-toes so that I could reach her neck. I wrapped both arms around her neck and bounced up and down. When I finished thanking her,

I ran and did the same to Dad. He kissed me on my cheek and whispered, "Proud of you."

Of course, I asked if I could tell Emma, Savannah, and Joey the news, and Mom and Dad agreed. I called Savannah first and then Dad helped me get Emma and Joey on the call as well. When I gave them the update, we all screamed and shouted. Our excitement was so loud through the speaker that I could barely understand anything anyone was saying. We celebrated for a few more minutes before saying goodbye.

While I was on the phone, Ashton and Amber convinced Mom and Dad to let us have a movie night. Since it was the weekend, they agreed. Ashton, Amber, and Ansley were already snuggled on the couch in their matching purple and blue striped one-piece pajamas. I ran to my room and found mine while calling for them to wait for me. I tossed my school clothes in the middle of my bedroom floor and dug out my one-piece from the bottom of my closet. Once I was dressed I reached in my school backpack and pulled out my black notebook.

"LENA!" I heard Ansley screaming my name down the hallway.

"Coming!" I replied. I quickly opened the notebook and found my to-do list. Right under the words "The Big Give" and next to the word "Date" I wrote May 2nd. Then I drew a gigantic checkmark across the entire page.

I knew we still had work to do but so many good things had happened today that I only wanted to focus on that. The list was still there, but being grateful for the checkmarks made everything seem possible!

Just one bite at a time, I said to myself and giggled while Ansley shouted my name again.

"Coming!" I yelled back while sliding down the hall in my polka dot socks as fast as I could. I dove onto the middle of the couch and landed right between my sisters.

Chapter 9

The next weeks were busier than I could have ever imagined. Mom and Dad knew that I was going to have a hard time staying focused so they helped me create a calendar with detailed to-do items on it. Dad explained that this was how he accomplished his busy weeks at work. On my calendar, he included the tasks for the event as well as everything else I had to do—like homework, spending time with God, and even spending time with family! Then he put little dates next to each. Those dates are when I needed to have certain things completed. There was also a place for me to mark when I actually completed each task. I tried to follow the schedule he created but it was hard.

Sometimes I would have a thought or idea that I wanted to work on even though it wasn't what was due. For example, I drafted a design for the advertising poster four days before it was scheduled and I turned in my history project two days early. Dad said staying ahead of the calendar was okay, but he encouraged me to never get behind. "You have too much to do and if you get behind it will be really hard to catch up," he insisted. I didn't want to find out for myself. I believed him and worked as hard as I could to stay on schedule.

His calendar helped me stay organized but my black notebook with my large checkmarks and doodles all over the pages was what I really loved looking at and using to help me plan. The pages filled with our lunch table notes made me smile.

We decided that every Friday night would be our family movie night. My sisters and I took turns choosing the movies we would watch and Mom would let us choose our meal. When it was my turn, instead of a movie we found a few kid's talent shows to watch while eating my favorite— taco soup! Amber chose a movie about horses, Ashton chose one with talking dogs, and Ansley chose her favorite mermaid story.

These nights quickly became my favorite time of the week. Things were going so quickly, and The Big Give was only one month away, but I loved spending time with my family. Relaxing and laughing with them made the busy and sometimes stressful Saturday workdays more fun.

Saturday afternoons at 1:00 were the best time for everyone to meet for our planning and work sessions, so that's what we ended up doing. Mom let us girls turn most of the game room into our workroom. She covered an old table with a brown paper tablecloth and filled three cups with pens, pencils, crayons, and markers. She also laid a large stack of paper in the middle of the table along with scissors and glue. She placed little matching notepads, a pen, and a bottle of water in front of every chair each Saturday. It looked like a real office and it made our meetings feel very important. Every Saturday, Savannah and Emma piled into the house in their gym shorts and non-matching T-shirts ready to work. Joey wore the same pair of striped leggings every week because during one meeting she accidently wrote on her leg with a hot pink permanent marker! Her mom was not happy about that and told her not to ruin any other clothes.

The adults we had helping us—Ms. Blount, Mom, Dad, and a few other teachers and friends from church and the neighborhood—met with us to see what we were doing with our checklist each week. Then they would move to the kitchen to discuss the more adult things like budgets, permits, and other details I really didn't know much about.

We all started every meeting together by praying just like the Fenways had when we filmed *Above the Waters*. When Dad was home he would read us a Scripture like he did after our family dinners in the evening. He loved talking to us about being kind to each other and the importance of asking God to help us no matter how big or small the task was. He said we needed to remember that we can do all things with God's help, and that even if things were getting difficult God would still help us. After we prayed we always played our favorite songs, usually Mallory Winston songs, and we would all jump right into our list of tasks.

By the third week of this routine I could tell that my friends were getting a little tired of all the lists and hard work. I tried to help everyone stay happy and motivated but I was feeling a little tired too.

Even deciding on the color of our flyer seemed like too difficult a task.

"Neon green," Emma said. "That way everyone will notice it."

Savannah sighed and with a bit of annoyance in her voice replied, "That is way too bright. It's a concert not a carnival."

"Emma has a point, though," Joey chimed in. "We do need everyone to notice it. We want people to be interested and to buy the tickets."

"Okay, guys, let's just choose a color so that we can move on. We still have to figure out where people will go to buy the tickets."

Emma threw her hands up in the air and flopped her elbows on top of the table. Her head landed in between her balled-up fists.

Mom must have heard the discussion because she walked right in holding her computer and smiling really big. "Hey, ladies, I have a surprise for you!" She was so excited that she was practically jumping up and down.

Amber, Ashton, and Ansley were two steps behind her and giggling.

"What is it?" I asked, sounding a little down.

Mom turned her computer to face us. "AHHHH!" Emma screamed first. "Mallory!"

"Hey, guys!" Mallory waved at us through the screen. "I hear you ladies have been working really hard!"

"Yes, we have!" I answered. Everyone else was too shocked to respond.

I reminded Mallory of who everyone was and introduced Joey. She remembered Emma and Savannah from their visit to California and she was excited to finally meet the newest member of our team.

"Joey! It's so fun to meet you!" she said.

Joey could not stop smiling and laughing. She just kept staring at the computer. I nudged her a little to break her silence. "Oh, uhhh, ooops . . . fun to meet you too!" she finally spoke.

"I am so happy to get to talk to you all! I have heard so many fabulous things about each of you," Mallory gushed. "I know I have already told Lena, but I want you to know that I am super proud of each of you! I wish I would have been so dedicated and caring about others when I was your age. You girls are truly amazing and are doing what God wants us all to do every day—show His love to others!"

We all smiled, nodded, and chuckled out the words, "Thank you."

"Okay! So what are you guys working on today?"

We looked down at the bright pieces of scrap paper we had just been arguing over and laughed.

"Well, actually, we could probably use your help," I said.

"Perfect, what is it?" Mallory look closely at the screen.

"We are designing the flyers . . . and well . . . we sort of can't agree on what color paper we should use," Emma admitted.

"Ooooh, great! I love making these types of decisions. So fun! What colors are you choosing from?"

Joey held up a few pieces of crumpled paper and play-fully let them fall onto the table in an even messier pile.

Mallory laughed so hard that she snorted. When Ansley heard her, she laughed even harder and squirted a little water from her nose. Mom shook her head and tried to stop herself from laughing. She didn't want Ansley to think that she approved. Emma saw Ansley and started imitating the face she made when she saw the water accidently drip from her nostrils. Before we knew it, laughter had taken over our meeting. We forgot our stress, the argument over the color of paper we should use, and everything else at that moment.

"I think we use them all!" Mom tried to compose herself again.

"Oh, yes! I love that." Mallory added, "Just print a certain amount on each color!"

Emma, Savannah, Joey, and I exchanged apologetic smiles and cheered. This was the perfect solution to our most recent issue.

Before ending our chat, Mom thanked Mallory for taking the time to talk to us and Mallory asked if she could pray with us.

We each grabbed onto the person's hand next to us and closed our eyes while Mallory prayed. "Dear God, thank you so much for the way that you orchestrate and plan out the details of our lives. I am so grateful for Lena and that a year ago she auditioned for the part in *Above the Waters*. God, that was something so fun. We can see how you have worked out the entire thing! Now, as Lena and her friends use their influence to help Caroline and the other children, we pray that you continue to work out all the details. Will you give them the energy they need, patience with each other, and all the resources needed to make this event a success? And I pray that they have fun and create wonderful memories together. In Jesus' name, amen."

As soon as she finished, Savannah said, "Thank you so much, Mallory!"

We all said goodbye and watched as Mallory disappeared from Mom's computer screen.

I ran over to Mom and placed my head on her shoulder. "Thank you, Mom! We needed that so much!"

She smoothed a piece of hair from my cheek and smiled. "I know."

"That was so cool!" Joey let out one last squeal.

I watched as Savannah's face shifted from a smile to a more serious look. I knew that she was ready to get back to work.

"Now that we know the colors of the flyers, maybe we should figure out exactly what information we want to include—like the cost of the event!" She couldn't stay serious for too long, though, and started laughing. "Or we could just hang a bunch of colorful pieces of paper around the school and neighborhood, with Mallory and Lena's pictures on them! Everyone would come!"

Once the laughter started again it was almost impossible for us to stop. We decided that was enough planning for the day. I told them that I would work with Ms. Blount to decide on the cost of the tickets and other important information we needed before we printed the flyers.

Everyone thought that sounded like a good idea, and we celebrated the end of the meeting with more smiles and rainbow-colored popsicles!

Chapter 10

It seemed as though every minute that I wasn't working on a school project, studying for a test, working on my at-home chores, or doing a massive amount of math homework, I was working on plans for The Big Give.

When Dad first added spending time with God to my calendar I didn't understand why it needed to be there. He always tells my sisters and me that reading our Bible should not be a chore. That we should do it because we want to spend time getting to know Him, like we do with our friends. When I told him that I didn't understand why it needed to be scheduled like all of my other tasks he explained. "Do you schedule sleepovers and time to practice for track?" he asked.

"Yes."

"Those aren't chores, but you schedule them to make sure you leave time for them. It's the same with spending time with God. It should never be a chore, but if it's something you want to do, then it helps if you have a planned time to do it."

Now that there were so many things going on, I was starting to understand what Dad was saying. So even though waking up earlier than my sisters so I could read the Bible and pray a little was getting harder and harder to do, I kept trying because I knew that I couldn't really do anything in my day without God's help.

The Monday morning after our Saturday flyer planning I dragged myself into the game room to read my Bible. As usual, Dad was already in there. I flopped down on the floor in front of him and closed my eyes.

Dad sat up in his chair and reached down. "Are you okay, Lena?" he asked in a very quiet voice.

I opened my eyes. When my eyes met Dad's, they filled with tears. "I am really tired," I said. "This is all a lot of work."

Dad pulled me up to my feet and sat me on his lap. "I know, Lena. Mom and I are doing as much as we can to help. We don't want you to feel like you are doing this all by yourself. Remember, you have friends that are helping—Ms. Blount, some of the other teachers, and all of your family. Just ask for more help if you need it."

I wiped my eyes and laid my head down on his chest. "I really feel like having this event is something God wanted me to do, but then sometimes I wonder if maybe I am wrong."

"Why is that?" Dad asked.

"Because it's so hard. Why would God want me to do something so hard?"

Dad let out a long sigh and gave me a tight squeeze. "Lena, remember when you were filming *Above the Waters* and you felt the same way? Like it was too hard?"

I nodded my head.

"Just because something is hard, doesn't mean that doing it is a mistake."

I sniffled and tried to keep the tears inside.

"The mistake would be trying to do hard things

without God's help. He gave you the opportunity to be in the movie, He gave you the opportunity to meet Caroline, and He gave you the desire to want to help her. Now let Him give you the strength and the help you need to do it."

As Dad continued to talk, I felt my body start to relax. I needed to hear his words and they were starting to make my heart feel better.

Dad reached next to him and grabbed his Bible. With arms still around me, he opened it in front my chest and read, "Philippians 4:6–7: 'Do not be anxious about anything, but in every situation, by prayer and petition, with thanksgiving, present your requests to God. And the peace of God, which transcends all understanding, will guard your hearts and your minds in Christ Jesus.'

"Lena, God doesn't want you to be overwhelmed. So if you need a break, let's take it. The rest of us can carry the load until you are feeling better! Young lady, we are in this together! Mom and I would not have let you even start this fundraising journey if we hadn't been ready and willing to help as much as possible."

Dad closed his Bible and set it back on the table.

"I am okay," I said. "I just forgot that I needed God's help. Thanks for the reminder, Dad."

I closed my eyes and fell back to sleep on Dad's lap until a wet kiss from Austin woke us both up a little while later.

Mom was already in the middle of fixing breakfast, so I rushed off to my room to get dressed for the day. Within 20 minutes everyone was dressed, finished eating, and standing in our family circle to pray. Dad read the same Scripture that he read to me earlier and reminded us all that as God's girls we don't have to worry about anything. Instead, we just need to pray and ask Him for help.

Even though I had just heard him say it, hearing it again, while holding my sisters' hands, made me feel even better.

Once I arrived at school I gathered Savannah, Emma, and Joey in the hall outside of Ms. Blount's classroom and told them about the Scripture Dad had read to me. It seemed as if it were helpful to me, then it would probably be helpful for each of us.

"Thanks, Lena. We definitely need to remember that," Savannah said.

"Yup!" Emma said in her usual chipper tone.

Joey stood quietly. "Does your dad always read the Bible to you guys?" she asked just before I turned to open the door to the classroom.

"Yes. Well, I try to read it on my own too, but he normally reads us a verse in the morning and we do a devotional together at night."

"Wow. I wish my dad did that." Joey looked sad.

"Well, you could always start reading it to him! Or maybe ask if you could tell him about one of the devotionals from the book I gave you while I was on tour," I suggested.

"I don't know," she said. She looked around a little at all of us and lowered her voice. "My family doesn't even go to church."

I blinked a few times and tried not to look surprised. I couldn't believe that I had never even asked Joey about her family. I didn't even know if she believed in God. "Oh, Joey! That's nothing to be embarrassed about." I grabbed her hand and swung it back and forth.

Joey smiled a little.

"I just feel weird sometimes. I've never really had friends that talked about God until I met you guys. Now sometimes I feel left out because I don't know or understand as much as you guys do. Since I don't go to church, I don't even know God."

"If you want, you can come with us sometimes! But going to church isn't what makes you know God. You know God by believing in Him and asking Him to be in charge of your life. Then the more time you spend learning about Him, the more you know Him."

Emma grabbed her other hand and said, "My family didn't always go to church, and they never used to talk about God until I was in the 4th grade! Now that's all they talk about!"

We all laughed.

"Joey, if you want, we can talk more during lunch today. This is way more important than anything else on our to-do list!"

"Okay. That sounds good." Joey looked happier.

The bell rang just as we were opening the door and taking our seats in our morning class with Ms. Blount. Ever since Ms. Blount started helping us with the event she seemed to smile just a little more when she saw us. As we walked by her desk, we each said, "Good morning, Ms. Blount," and took our seats.

As we got closer to lunchtime, I wasn't thinking about the normal list of things we needed to talk about. Instead, I was thinking about Joey and how I could help her. My family had always gone to church, and I didn't always remember that not every dad was like mine. I didn't want her to feel bad or weird around us. I really wanted her to know that God loved her and she didn't have to feel weird. If God could help us plan this event, then I knew he could help Joey's family too.

Now that we were in the final weeks before The Big Give, Ms. Blount agreed to let us have lunch in her room every Monday and Thursday in order to work with her on some of the final details. This was perfect because being alone in her room would give us a chance to really talk to Joey and to maybe even pray for her.

Like always, we grabbed our lunches as quickly as we could and made our way back to the classroom. Ms. Blount was busy strolling the aisles in the cafeteria so we were all alone.

There were a few moments of awkward silence before Savannah asked Joey if she was okay and if she had any more questions about God.

"No, I am just really glad I know you guys. Maybe one day my dad will want to go to church. But at least right now I get to learn from you guys."

"Well, we don't know it all but we are glad to help you however we can!" Emma said.

I cleared my throat and tried to sound brave when I asked, "Can I ask you a question?"

"Yup," Joey said while taking a bite out her of peanut butter and jelly sandwich.

"Do you believe in God and God's son, Jesus?"

Joey put her sandwich down and looked at me. I wasn't sure what she was going to say. I didn't mean to make her upset, so I smiled and pretended to look at my lunch.

"I don't know if I did before, but I do now. I think even watching your movie, *Above the Waters*, helped me a lot." She thought for a moment. "And I've always loved Mallory Winston's songs and they talk about God. But after learning more about her and getting to talk to her at your house, it all really made me want to know more."

"Aw, that's great!" Savannah cheered.

"Can we pray for you?" I asked.

Joey nodded her head yes. I closed my eyes and even though I wasn't sure what to pray, I did it anyway. I remembered praying for my tour bus driver, Mr. Ernie, and decided I would do the same thing.

"Dear God, thank you for Joey. I am glad that you have made her our friend! I know that she believes in you and wants to learn more about you. Please, will you help her to know how much you love her? In Jesus' name, amen."

When we opened our eyes Joey had a tear rolling down her cheek. She quickly wiped it away and smiled.

"Soooo, how about that budget? How much are we charging for tickets and VIP tickets and T-shirts?" Emma said playfully. We all laughed as the atmosphere around us got a little less serious.

"Thanks for the reminder on that stuff! I'll ask Mom and Dad to talk to Ms. Blount about that if they haven't already. I think we've done all we can handle for today!"

Chapter 11

I did just what I said I was going to do. That evening I asked Mom and Dad to work with Ms. Blount on creating the price list while Emma, Savannah, Joey, and I continued to work on some of the other details.

Dad agreed and met with Ms. Blount the next day.

As we sat around the kitchen table together that evening, Mom and Dad told me everything that they decided with Ms. Blount. Together they decided that we should charge $35 for a regular ticket to the event. We would charge $55 for a VIP ticket, which meant that person got to actually meet Mallory for a few minutes after the show.

Dad took the last bite of his chicken and said, "Ms. Blount thought it was a good idea to have the ticket cost include a T-shirt. That way people will only have to spend money one time. Mom and I agreed. I think we will raise more that way. And we will figure out a way that the ticket holders can still choose their T-shirt color. And they can buy additional T-shirts, of course."

"We think you can get about 1,500 people to come to the concert," Mom said while still concentrating on her dinner.

"That's a lot of people!" I exclaimed. I had to admit that that was a lot more people than I was expecting, although we hadn't talked about it too much.

"Yes, it is. But to raise $150,000 you will need a lot

more than that. That's only about $52,000. We will have to really try to get a lot of things donated in order to take care of the costs of supplies and still raise money." Dad wiped his napkin across his top lip. He didn't sound very hopeful.

I knew that $150,000 sounded like a lot of money but I really believed we could do it. "I'll just keep talking to God about it," I said, trying to stay positive. "He'll help us."

Dad tilted his head a little to the right and smiled a little.

"Mallory has a lot of fans!" Mom added. "I think there could be a huge turnout, especially now that the movie has had so much success. And people love to see you two together. Maybe we will have even more than 1,500 show up!"

Ansley grunted. "All of those people can't fit in your school, Lena!" Ansley added to the conversation.

"Oh, that reminds me. Mr. Fraser agreed to let us have it outside on the big field next to your building." Dad pushed his chair back from the table and stood up. "Forgot to tell you that. When we realized just how big this event could get, we needed to think about alternatives and the field seemed the best option. It's huge and level and can certainly accommodate that many."

He walked over to the counter and picked up his Bible. We all knew that meant it was time for our family devotional.

"Daddy," I interrupted him right before he started reading the Scripture he had opened his Bible to. "Joey was sad today," I said. "Her dad doesn't read the Bible, and they don't go to church either."

"Aww, that's so sad." Amber sat up on her knees.

"Does she know God?" Ansley asked while sliding her

hand under the table to give Austin a little taste of dinner. He licked her fingers while I explained everything that had happened with Joey.

Dad told me that I did the right thing by telling her how much God loves her and inviting her to church with us. He also said we should make praying for her a part of our family's prayer time.

"I'm glad you talked to her, Lena, and I am glad you are talking about it with us." He took a sip of water, and Mom added, "Girls, it's very important that we go to church and learn about God as a family. The reason we do that is not just so we can make our lives better or more fun, but so we can tell others! Never make your friends feel bad about not knowing God. Instead, be willing to be the one to tell them more."

"So, Mommy," Ashton perked up. "What if we have friends that don't want to know God?"

"Well, you can't make a person want to know God. All you can do is tell them, and show them what knowing God looks like."

"Huh?" Ansley finally raised her hand from Austin's mouth and wiped them on her napkin.

"Gross!" I shouted.

"Girls," Dad said with a stern voice to get our attention. "This is important. Listen to Mom."

Mom smiled and reached for Dad's Bible. She opened up to Galatians 5:22–23 and read, "But the fruit of the Spirit is love, joy, peace, forbearance, kindness, goodness, faithfulness, gentleness and self-control. Against such things there is no law."

She closed the Bible and scanned the table until she was sure she had our attention. "You can show others what knowing God is like by showing His fruit."

"Ooohhhh! I get it." Amber said the words like a song.

"What kind of fruit grows on an apple tree?" Mom asked.

"Apples!" Ashton was the first one to respond.

"What kind of fruit grows on a cherry tree?"

"Cherries!" Amber's word raced out.

"So, if you're like a Jesus tree, what kind of fruit should you grow?"

No one rushed to answer.

Dad started us off. "We are love, joy, peace . . ."

All of us said each of the fruits Mom had read until we named all nine of them.

"Exactly!" Mom said, full of enthusiasm. "I love seeing the fruit you girls grow!"

This wasn't the first time we had heard about the fruit of the Spirit, but it seemed to make more sense this time.

"One more thing." Dad leaned back in his seat. "Does anyone like to eat rotten fruit?"

"Nope." Ashton frowned.

"So don't be rotten to each other or to your friends."

The dinner table quickly filled with laughter. "You don't be rotten!" Ashton pointed a playful finger at me. "No! You better not be rotten . . . yuck!" I laughed and started teasing each of my sisters.

Mom and Dad stood and started clearing the table and we joined them.

"Okay, girls, time to get ready for bed! School tomorrow," Dad said.

We all hurried down the hall to our rooms joking and teasing each other along the way. After we took our showers Mom and Dad tucked each of us in and turned off the lights.

"Lena?" Ansley whispered. "Even if you don't make enough money to help Caroline, at least you helped Joey."

I smiled. Ansley was right. I closed my eyes and thanked God for helping me to grow and be fruit for others.

Chapter 12

Once Mr. Fraser agreed to let us have the event outside, we had a brand-new list of tasks we needed to accomplish. I told Savannah, Emma, and Joey the news. Now there was more to panic about.

"What about the weather?" asked Savannah, as always the practical one. "It's spring and that's storm season in Dallas. We cannot control that!"

I told them not worry. "We just need to add that to the list of things we are already praying for," I said. But that made me a little nervous too.

Dad helped me create a list of items we needed. He said we now needed to rent a stage, tables, and chairs. Since The Big Give was set for May, we didn't worry too much about it being too cold in Dallas. However, Ms. Blount did suggest that we rent large tents in case it rained. She told us we could have the stage under some type of covering as well as the T-shirts and food under another. We all agreed that was a good idea and added the cost to the growing list of expenses.

Then Mom had a great idea. "Maybe I'll call Mallory and Sammy. They must have some type of stage and covering they use on the road for outdoor concerts. They may be willing to let us use their structure for the fundraiser. It could save us lots of money!"

Dad asked us to write a letter that he could use when

asking for donations. Ms. Blount agreed to help us girls. She helped us explain our needs and suggested we also include pieces of Caroline and the other families' stories as well as Mallory's biography as part of the perfect letter to ask for help.

Dad took the letter to where he worked, and they agreed to donate enough to pay for the tent rentals! They wanted to be called our sponsor and asked that we hang their company banner on the stage. Of course, no one had a problem with that, and we celebrated the response.

After realizing how easy it was to use the letter to ask for help, we came up with a list of other places to go and ask for donations. Mom took it with her to our local grocery stores and they agreed to donate hotdogs, buns, chips, and bottles of water. Another store donated paper plates, napkins, and cookies to sell.

Every time we received a new donation I remembered the morning I sat on Dad's lap and he told me not to be anxious but to ask for help. The more we stopped trying to do everything ourselves, the more help God seemed to send!

Ms. Blount asked our art teacher, Mr. Shipply, if he would be willing to help us put the final touches on the flyer and the T-shirt designs. With only four weeks before the event he agreed to stay after school on Friday evenings to help us with any design work that we needed. Emma, Joey, and Savannah had track practice so Mom came with Amber, Ashton, and Ansley.

The first thing we needed to do was finish the flyers. Now that we had all the information, we could fill in the cost, the date, the time, the location, and exactly how to get

in touch with the school office (who had generously volunteered to handle the sale of the tickets), and who would be
at the concert. It was easy to fill in the blank spaces. Mr.
Shipply made them look super fun with a picture of Mallory
standing with one hand on her hip and the other waving in
the air. When she saw it, Emma said it looked like she was
jumping off the flyer and telling people, "Hello!"

Once they were complete and the team approved,
including Mallory, Mom took a copy to our church and
asked if they would print 3,000 copies of the flyer. When
she showed them our letter and explained what we were
doing, they offered to print them for free.

When Mom brought them home we all screamed! They
were so pretty! We all spent the rest of the week passing
them out to everyone in our school and taping copies of
them on bathroom doors everywhere we went! People
even offered to help us distribute them all around Dallas,
and we needed even more copies, which the church was
happy to help with.

By the end of the week we were amazed at how much
had been accomplished and by how many things were
donated to our fundraising efforts. We used our Saturday
work time to pass out more flyers in our neighborhoods, and
we took stacks of them to a few churches and restaurants.

"With this many flyers I don't think you will have a
problem getting at least 1,500 people to show up!" Mom's
confidence was contagious. We all believed her and were
excited by the thought.

The next week was dedicated to helping Mr. Shipply
finalize the design for the T-shirts. We finally decided it

was best if each shirt looked exactly the same except for the shirt color and the family name that was being supported. Caroline's shirt was turquoise because that was my favorite color. The others were purple, fuchsia, lime green, and tie-dye. Each name would be printed across the middle in large white bubble-type letters. Ms. Blount had given us the great news that a local screen printing company had offered to donate the T-shirts for our fundraiser! This was an amazing gift. The whole team decided that besides getting a T-shirt with each ticket sold we would have extras printed to sell for $10 each. We ordered 500 extra—100 of each color. Mr. Shipply said that having the shirts in different colors was a good idea because we could make it a fun competition on the night of the show, seeing which color was the most popular. We all loved that idea and thanked him for helping us.

Since the school was helping out so much, Mr. Fraser asked if the school could sponsor the T-shirts, and we, of course, agreed. He only asked that we put our school banner outside of the tent where the shirts and food would be sold. We loved that idea because that was also near where Mallory would set up a booth to sign autographs and meet people.

When I asked Mr. Shipply how he would get our designs off the paper and onto a shirt he suggested we take the artwork to the printer and see the process for ourselves.

That week mom agreed to drive us to the printer during our Saturday meeting.

Joey showed up in her workout leggings as always and Emma and Savannah wore their gym shorts. I thought

about putting on a pair of nice jeans in order to look profes-
sional but quickly decided against the idea when I saw my
friends. We piled into the van and followed the directions
Mr. Shipply had given us.

When we pulled up to the building we thought we
were at the wrong address. The building was brown with
a red metal door and an old black fence that only wrapped
around a part of the building. There was only one car in
the parking lot and the place looked empty. Mom glanced
down at her phone at the directions again, then looked
closely at the building.

"Are you sure Mr. Shipply gave you the right address,
Mom?" I asked.

"I'm not sure I want to get out, Mrs. Daniels," Savannah
said cautiously.

"I think this is it, girls," she said back, just as cautiously.
"Stay with me." She gathered her things and got out of
the van.

Emma looked at us and shrugged. Then she slid the
back door open and jumped out.

We stayed two steps behind Mom and walked up to
the door. When she rang the bell a girl opened the door
with a huge smile on her face.

She didn't look very old and was wearing a pair of gym
shorts and a T-shirt, just like us.

"Hi, guys! You must be the Daniels family and friends,
right?"

She swung the door open wide and welcomed us in.

Mom introduced herself first and then turned to each
of us.

The young, bouncy girl shook our hands and said, "I'm Trina! This is my mom and dad's T-shirt printing company and I work for them."

Emma secretly tugged my hand a little and I knew it meant that she was excited. I smiled in agreement. The building looked completely different on the inside than it did on the outside. The walls were each painted a different color with brightly colored artwork hanging all around. There was a long white couch facing the door and a tiny white metal desk sitting in the corner. It smelled like a bag of lemons and the soft music playing reminded me of being in an elevator.

"Come this way, everyone," Trina said.

Trina took us into the back of the print shop where there were machines lined against the walls. She explained what each of them did and walked us to the supply closet. "This is where we keep all of the different shirts. I think we have a note of which colors you want but let me know if it looks like I pulled the wrong ones."

She went behind a door and rolled out a huge basket of shirts. Immediately, I could see all the colors we chose and told her that it all looked right.

She and Mom went over all the details—sizes, spelling of the names, and quantities of each. Once everything was agreed upon, she asked if Mom could put her initial by the order to show that we approved.

Mom handed me the pen and I slowly wrote "L.D."

Next we watched Trina hook up the computer and turn on the machines. She played with a few buttons, made a few adjustments, and hit a big green button.

Slowly we started hearing the machines rumble. "Alright, it's all set! It will take them a few hours to run, so you can pick them up tomorrow."

Mom nodded. "Thank you so much, Trina. And please, thank your parents for their donation of the shirts and printing." She walked us back out toward the front of the building.

Trina stopped at the desk, picked up a white envelope, and handed it to Joey. Joey handed it to Mom.

"We want you to know that my family loved *Above the Waters*. It was such a good movie," Trina said, looking directly at me.

I was shocked and a little embarrassed by her words. I felt everyone look in my direction, so I smiled as wide as I could and said thank you.

"So anyway, when my parents heard all about what you guys are doing for these children and their families they really wanted to help. We won't be able to make the concert in two weeks, but please add this gift from us to your donations as well." She pointed at the white envelope Mom was holding.

"Wow!" Emma shouted.

"That's so awesome!" Joey added.

"Thank you so much!" Mom and I both reached out to hug her.

"Praying for you guys! And you can pick up your shirts after 2:00 p.m. tomorrow."

"We will come right after church."

We each said thank you again and walked back out the big red metal door.

All of us girls raced to the van and climbed in. "Open it! Mom, please, open it!"

So Mom chuckled and ripped open the end of the envelope. There was light blue check in there with my name on it. I looked over Mom's shoulder as she held it up. "Five thousand dollars!" I shouted, which eventually turned into a scream, and ended in a cry and tears of happiness.

Emma, Joey, Savannah, and Mom all celebrated too.

"They know God too! He really is helping us!" Joey squealed and Mom replied, "Yes, He is!"

After such a fun and amazing day, I asked if my friends could sleep over and go to church with us in the morning. I didn't want the celebration to end! Mom agreed and everyone called their parents to ask for permission.

"What about our clothes? I don't have any church clothes," Joey asked quickly.

"We are all about the same size. You can all wear some of mine!"

That night before bed we turned my closet into a little boutique. Tossing shoes to each other, trying on skirts and pants while holding up matching shirts to see what looked best. Amber, Ansley, Ashton, and even Austin were the judges and guided our decisions for our Sunday morning attire.

We woke up bright and early the next morning, dressed quickly, and made our way to church. Joey watched everything with her eyes wider than usual. She laughed, smiled, and read all the words to the songs off the screen so that she could sing along.

After church, when Mom and Dad asked her what she

thought, she couldn't stop smiling. "I loved it! I'm going to pray that God helps my dad to come too!"

I was just as happy about Joey's excitement about church as I was with the large boxes of T-shirts we picked up after services.

That night I prayed and thanked God for the donations, my family, and my friends.

Chapter 13

"One week left! One week left!" Emma chanted as she marched off the school bus and into the building. The weather had been hot and stormy lately and her hair was pulled up into one big curly ponytail and bounced with every word she shouted.

Joey and I just shook our heads and followed her into the building.

We saw Savannah standing in front of her locker as soon we turned down the hall. We all waved and rushed over to her.

"Hey!" she greeted us.

"One week left!" Emma chanted again.

"Yes, that means we have a lot of work to do!" I said.

Even though our to-do list pages were almost completely covered in checkmarks, there was still so much to do.

"I'm not worried about it though. We just need to put some things on our calendar and get them all done before Saturday morning!"

"We can do that at lunch. I think we need to add praying for good weather. Mom said the forecast is looking rainy—storms could be headed this way," Savannah said just as the bell rang for the school day to begin.

We piled into Ms. Blount's classroom and said, "Good morning."

"This is a big week for you, ladies," she said as we took

our seats. "I asked Mr. Shipply to help with lunch this week so that I can meet with you in here. Be on time. We have a lot to get done."

Ms. Blount turned and welcomed everyone else to homeroom.

The morning seemed extra-long, but it was eventually lunchtime, of course, so we did what we were told. We left our Spanish class, grabbed our lunches, and headed straight back to Ms. Blount's room. She was waiting for us, and even though we weren't late, it felt like it. So, we apologized anyway.

Ms. Blount was sitting behind her desk and told each of us to pull up a chair. She started talking right away. "So, I met with Mr. Fraser this morning and . . ." She took a bite of her apple and chewed slowly. We sat on the edge of our seats waiting for her to finish. She held up one finger indicating that we needed to be patient.

When she finished chewing, she started again. "Okay, I talked to Mr. Fraser. After the busy weekend of ticket sales, he said we have officially sold 1,452 tickets."

My mouth dropped open as wide as it could and I could not breathe.

"No way!!" Joey shouted.

Ms. Blount simply nodded her head, a pleased and proud expression on her face. "You ladies did a wonderful job advertising for this event. Well done."

We all could not stop giggling and celebrating Ms. Blount's news.

"So . . . I asked Mr. Shipply if he would draw a map of the field outside." She reached in her drawer and pulled out a piece of construction paper with a pencil drawing of the outside of our school on it. "We need to look at this and decide how we to want to set everything up outside on the field."

She set the paper in the middle of the desk and told us to brainstorm. We each had a different opinion about where the two tents and the stage with its overhead structure should go, but after talking it through, we came to a decision. We placed little marks all over the drawing so that we would remember and be able to tell the people helping us set up.

"Well," Ms. Blount said as she wiped a few crumbs from her desk into her hands. "That's about it for today. We will do this again every day this week just to make sure we have a good game plan for Saturday. Have you ladies assigned yourselves jobs yet, for the day of the event?"

We looked at each other and back at her.

"Uhhhhh . . ."

"Oh, no. Okay, let's do that quickly. Joey, I think you need to be a floater. That means you work out in the crowd and if people have questions or look confused you can help guide them to where they need to be. We have a lot of parent volunteers that agreed to help you with this too. Your energy, smile, and excitement will help everyone feel welcome and taken care of."

Next she turned to Emma. "Would you like to be the MC?"

"The what?" Emma asked politely.

"MC is another way of saying the host. Would you like to host the event? Welcome everyone, introduce Mallory Winston up on stage ..."

"YES! Of course!"

"Savannah, I think you would be great at helping manage that sales tent of ours. Work with the volunteers to pass out the shirts to ticketholders and selling the others, keep all the sizes organized, find Lena and Mallory when it's time for them to be on stage, etc. How's that sound?"

"Perfect. I was praying you didn't ask me to be on the stage! I like working behind the scenes."

Ms. Blount smiled just a little. She knew us all pretty well.

"Lena, you can talk to Mallory about the best way to do this, but you both need to thank everyone for coming, tell the story behind the event, and share why you felt the need to do this. Okay?"

"Yes!"

Just then the bell rang. "Okay, clean up your places and get ready for your next class. We will talk more tomorrow. Be on time."

We each hopped up and did exactly what we were told. I was grateful for all of Ms. Blount's help and I was starting to really like being around her. When I told Savannah, Emma, and Joey that, they all laughed and agreed.

"She must like teaching middle school better!" Emma said.

"Yeah, she wasn't that nice when she taught at our old school." I turned and spoke directly to Joey.

Savannah interrupted us and said, "Well, maybe we just didn't take the time to notice. I think sometimes we thought she was being mean when she wasn't really. I like her."

I had to agree. "Good point, Savannah. Good point." I patted her on the shoulder and scurried past her. I was feeling extra energetic and wanted to let a little of it out before class.

Chapter 14

Tuesday, Wednesday, and Thursday zoomed by and somehow I managed to stay focused during math, history, science, and all of my other classes. Every night I made sure I thanked God for helping me to do that.

On Thursday afternoon Mr. Fraser and Mr. Shipply joined our lunch meeting with Ms. Blount. They looked over all of our plans and notes for the big day. Mr. Fraser read the program out loud to make sure everything sounded good. Once he approved we quickly moved onto the short list of tasks that still needed to be accomplished.

"Someone needs to be here Saturday morning when the rental company comes to set up the tents and Mallory's crew comes to put the stage up. Have you already asked anyone to do that?" Mr. Fraser asked.

"Yes! My mom and dad will be here," I answered. "Also a few other parents offered to be on stand-by."

"And Mallory will come for a sound check three hours before the event starts to make sure everything is set up properly for her," Joey answered.

Mr. Fraser looked impressed with the details we were able to offer. Then he scanned the list to see what else was missing.

"Mr. Shipply? Do you have anything to add?"

"Uh, yes." Mr. Shipply cleared his throat a little. "We need to organize the tickets so that we have a color system that matches with the shirts they get. I can help you ladies do that on Friday—tomorrow evening. We can meet right after school."

"Uh-oh," Savannah said.

"Ohhh, yeah," Joey mumbled.

"Track. We have track," Emma finished each of their thoughts.

Mr. Shipply shifted a little in his seat while he thought of a way to make it work.

"Well, Lena, can you be here? Ms. Blount will be here as well. It would be nice to have as many hands on deck as possible."

"I can come. I am sure I can bring my sisters, Amber, Ansley, and Ashton too. They have been a part of the team and would love to help more, I'm sure! I could bring my dog . . . but . . ."

Emma let out one of her loud hardy laughs. "Austin would be a disaster! He may not be helpful but he would make everyone laugh!"

Mr. Shipply smiled at Emma's contagious laughter. "Okay, well, let's leave the dog home, but ask your mom to bring your sisters. And tell them to come ready to work!"

I was a little disappointed that Savannah, Emma, and Joey would not be able to join us but I knew that my sisters would love being able to help too.

After the meeting, Savannah stood up and came right over to me. "I am really sorry, Lena. I know Friday is a big night with a lot to do. I am sorry we can't be here."

"Do you think we should miss track practice?" Joey asked.

"We can't. Not if we want a good shot at making the track team. Remember, coach said he needed to see how serious we were?"

I tried not to look too disappointed. "It's okay, guys. I wouldn't want you to miss it! I know you would if you could, but we will be fine!"

I knew that asking them to skip practice would not have been fair. They had spent just as much time planning this event as I had and they didn't even know Caroline. I was grateful for all they had done.

"I'm sure my mom will bring us all early Saturday morning so that we can finish everything else!" Savannah attempted to change the discussion to something more positive.

"What time is Mallory coming?" Joey asked. "I don't want to be all sweaty when I meet her!"

"Well, anything's better than when I met her the first time—I had gum in my hair!"

"Ohhhh, yeah!!" Emma remembered hearing the story. "That must have been totally embarrassing. But it shows how nice she really is because she's still your friend!"

After that, Joey had many questions about how I actually got the part in the movie and what it was like to meet Mallory. I used our last few minutes before math to tell her about it. I had been so busy planning the event that I really had forgotten about it. No one really treated me differently anymore and it had been a long time since anyone asked me for an autograph. Emma said that was only because I was spending all of my time in Ms. Blount's classroom.

"Good point, Emma. Good point."

We all laughed and sprinted to class.

When I finally made it home, the first thing I did was find my sisters to tell them that I needed their help. "Ansley!" I called out, and they all came running to greet me at the door like I knew they would. "Guys, I need your help."

They all leaned in close and waited to hear what I needed them to do. I told them what Mr. Shipply had told us at our lunch meeting and watched as their faces brightened.

"Can we have a shirt?!" Amber was so tickled she could barely stand still.

"Of course," Mom approved from in the kitchen. "Okay now, ladies. Let's get your homework done and get ready for dinner—taco soup!"

"YES!" I shouted and scurried off as fast as I could.

At the end of the day, I pulled out my little black notebook and looked over my messy pages of checkmarks. I also pulled out the calendar and schedule Dad had created for me and smiled. There were so many dates that had passed and somehow we'd managed to accomplish what we planned to do.

Now all I needed was to force myself to sleep. This day had been filled with so many wonderful things. I fell asleep with a smile plastered across my face.

Chapter 15

"One more day! One more day!" Emma chanted every chance she got. On the bus, walking down the hall, waiting for class to start, and before our lunch meeting. She didn't stop until Ms. Blount walked into the room.

"Nice to see you ladies on time today," she said as her long dress swooshed across the floor.

Ms. Blount took her seat at the table and looked at each us. "I don't believe I have ever been prouder of a group of students." The little creases in the corner of her eye started to moisten. She inhaled and held the tears in.

We all just sat quietly. We had never seen Ms. Blount show emotion like this, and listening to her tell us how proud of us she was really meant a lot.

"I have loved every moment of watching you learn, persevere, and work so hard for someone else. I don't know how much money you will end up raising tomorrow, but I want you to know that the work you have done and the example you set for your peers and your school are priceless. You remind me so much of Bethany Pickney, Andrew Tatem, and Suzanne Stephens. I cannot wait to see what other amazing things you girls do for those around you."

Ms. Blount finally let herself smile. It was soft and pretty. Her lips curled just a little in the corners and her top lip rested on her two front teeth.

I could hear a few sniffles coming from Emma. Her

sniffles were just as contagious as her smile, and we each tried to hold back our tears but we just couldn't.

Ms. Blount cleared her throat and waited a few seconds before reaching into her bag and pulling out her lunch. "Let's eat, girls. There are still many things to discuss before tomorrow."

Ms. Blount may have been right but we couldn't think of any. Everything seemed to be in place and ready to go. Our brains were ready for a break.

So while we ate, we talked a little bit about Saturday morning and a lot about Mallory Winston. Ms. Blount did not know any of her music so Emma and Joey attempted to sing a few of their favorites. Ms. Blount listened but no matter how hard they tried or how silly they sounded they could not get another smile from her. It didn't matter though because we all knew she was happy on the inside.

As we were finishing up our last lunch meeting, Ms. Blount had one more thing. "Girls, we had the screen printer design special T-shirts for you and the rest of the volunteers. Let me get yours."

She stood and went to her desk where a stack of colorful T-shirts were neatly folded and waiting. Each was a different color and ours were extra special. While all the T-shirts for the volunteers had STAFF printed across the backs, ours had our names on them as well! These were T-shirts we would all keep for a very long time.

After school, Emma, Savannah, and Joey apologized again for not being able to help Mr. Shipply and me with the shirts. "It's okay, guys!" I promised them and told them to have fun.

As I watched them rush off to track practice, I felt a tiny lump form in my throat. I wasn't sure if it was because I wanted to run track or just because I wanted to be with my friends. I shook my head and tried to focus my attention on how important and how much fun our weekend was going to be.

I waited in the office for Mom to arrive with my sisters. When I saw them walking up from the parking lot in their gym shorts and mismatched T-shirts I smiled. When I looked closer, I realized they were all wearing shorts and shirts that used to be mine. Ansley was wearing my favorite pair of royal blue shorts with little green circles on them and an orange T-shirt from my 5th grade spirit day. She was holding Ashton's hand and skipping ahead of Mom and Amber. I jumped up to meet them at the door and led them straight to Mr. Shipply's classroom.

"Hello, Daniels girls and Mrs. Daniels." He waved and flashed a jolly smile. Mom nudged them softly on the shoulders, and they each introduced themselves.

When they saw the shirts their eyes widened and they were ready to work.

Mr. Shipply gave us each very specific instructions, including Mom, and told us to get started. We moved boxes across the room to the wall near the door, ready to take out to the field in the morning. We also refolded shirts and stacked them by size to create a system to easily let people choose the family they wanted to show support for. Mr. Shipply told the girls to go and choose their T-shirts so that they could take them home and have them to wear in the morning. Ashton, Amber, and Ansley each chose the one with Caroline's name going across the front. I had not talked to her since we first decided to help, and I could not wait to let her know how much we were able to accomplish for her in our community.

After we finished with the T-shirts, Mr. Shipply asked Mom if we had time to go outside and take a final look at the set-up plan. He wanted to be extra sure that the plans were just right before everyone and everything started arriving in the morning. With the weather forecast the way it was, we were hoping the rain would hold off and that set-up would go without a hitch.

"Of course!" Mom agreed.

Ansley, Ashton, and Amber ran ahead of us. A part of me really wanted to race my sisters but I decided it was best to stay close to Mom and Mr. Shipply just to make sure I didn't miss anything they discussed.

As we approached the door leading out to the big field, Ansley was headed back in our direction.

"Lena! Lena!" she was screaming. "It's Emma! Hurry up!"

"What? What is it?" Mom said frantically, moving as fast as she could out the door too.

"I think she hurt herself! She's on the track." Ansley was pointing to a big crowd of 6th and 7th grade runners.

We moved as quickly as we could through the crowd. I could hear Emma crying before I could see what was going on. Mom and Mr. Shipply scattered the other kids away so that they could talk to the coach and find out what happened and what needed to be done.

"I'll call her mother," Mom said, while dropping her large brown purse to the ground in order to dig out her phone.

"An ambulance is already on the way," the coach announced calmly.

Emma cried out in pain again. I knelt next to her and laid my face next to hers. I repeated, "It's okay, Emma, it's okay," over and over until Mom told me I needed to make space for the paramedics. "It's okay, Emma. It's okay," I whispered one last time.

Mom did her best to keep calm because she knew that Ansley, Ashton, Amber, and I were watching her to determine how scared we should be.

"It's okay, guys. It's just her knee. We can't tell how bad it is, but she will be fine." Mom guided us to the parking lot while she talked. "I told her mom we would meet her at the hospital."

"But Mommy, why couldn't she just wait for her mom?" Amber asked as we loaded in the van in a slight panic.

"She could have but she is in a lot of pain. She needs to see a doctor very soon and an ambulance can drive faster than a regular car."

Mom drove faster than I had ever seen her drive. She asked me to dial Dad's number on the way to tell him what happened. I put him on speakerphone. "Let's pray for her," he said.

Everyone but Mom closed their eyes.

"Dear God, we pray that you would comfort Emma now. We pray that you give the doctors wisdom to know just what they need to do. We pray that you keep her mother and father safe as they drive to the hospital and that they would not be worried. Help us all to trust you right now. We know you are in charge. In Jesus' name, amen."

"Amen."

"Okay, honey, let me know when you get there. I can leave work to meet you at the hospital if I need to," Dad said before hanging up.

We pulled into the parking lot at the same time as Emma's mom was walking in. Mom pulled up to the front of the hospital and told me I could go in and help Emma's mom find where they had taken her. I jumped out and ran into the hospital, catching up to Emma's mom. She looked worried and very flustered. Her cheeks were red and she had little drops of sweat rolling down her nose. When we entered the large lobby, coach immediately saw us and hurried over. He motioned for me to have a seat while he talked to Emma's mom privately.

I kept my eyes glued to the door waiting for Mom to come in. She came in along with Joey, Savannah, and Savannah's mom. I didn't know why but seeing their faces gave me a little bit of relief. I jumped up and ran to Savannah. I wrapped my arms around her neck and asked her to tell me what happened. Neither she nor Joey really knew. They said the team was doing sprints when suddenly they heard Emma screaming out in pain.

"Somebody said they thought Emma tripped and fell. I heard someone else say they thought they saw a bone sticking out of Emma's leg!" said Joey, who looked worried and a little sick to her stomach too.

When Savannah's mom heard Joey say that, she interrupted. "Okay, guys, that's probably not true. We will find out what really happened soon. Just take a seat."

As I sat there waiting to see what the adults had to say,

a lot of "what ifs" starting racing through my head. I was very worried about my friend, but there was a part of me that could not stop worrying about what we would do at The Big Give without her help. I felt selfish for thinking about it and I tried not to. No one else said anything, but I could not help but wonder if I was the only one.

We had been sitting in the waiting room for what felt like hours. Dad had come and taken Ansley, Ashton, and Amber home by then, but Mom said she would wait with me to find out how Emma was doing. I glanced down at my watch and as I looked up, I saw my mom talking to one of the nurses. The rumbles of thunder we had started hearing while waiting were adding to my already stretched nerves.

They whispered for a while and then the nurse said, "Savannah, Joey, and Lena? Emma would like to see you. She's doing much better now."

I jumped up from my seat and practically ran to the door with the other girls. We nervously followed the nurse down the long hallway and into a room on a corner of the hall.

Emma was sort of sitting up with her leg hanging in the air from a pole. She tried to smile when she saw us but I could tell she wasn't feeling well.

"We gave her some medicine to help with the pain. They make her feel really sleepy too," said the nurse before stepping back so we could get closer to Emma's bed.

"Hey," I said while rubbing her hand. Savannah stood next to me, and Joey walked to the other side.

"I'm so sorry," Joey leaned in close and spoke directly

into Emma's ear. I knew that Emma's tears were contagious and, before I could stop myself, my eyes filled with tears of my own. Even though I knew Emma was going to be okay, it was difficult to see her this way.

"Can we pray for you?" I asked.

Joey quickly said, "Can I do it?"

Emma nodded her head weakly.

We stood quietly as Joey prayed that God would help Emma feel better. When she finished, we were all in tears.

"Okay, Lena, we need to get home. Emma needs to rest and tomorrow is a big day for all of us." Mom's voice startled me. I didn't even know she had come into the room.

"Alright." I rubbed Emma's hand one more time, smiled, and told her I'd see her tomorrow. I didn't know if that was true but I prayed it was.

Chapter 16

As Mom and I walked out to the van with Savannah, her mother, and Joey, lightning flashed and thunder rumbled in the distance again.

"I hope this all blows right over town," Mom said, her hair whipping around in the wind that suddenly seemed to be increasing in speed. "It'll make it difficult to set things up in the morning if the field is covered in puddles and mud from a downpour."

"Mom! Don't even think about it! I don't know what we would do . . ." I groaned as Savannah, Joey, and I gave a group hug to each other and got into our vehicles to get home. It had been a long day and we were all still worried about Emma.

As we drove away, all waving out the windows and calling, "Good night!" the rain started splattering against the windshield and I saw Mom shake her head a little. "Don't worry, Lena. The wind will blow this through quickly. Or at least it will dry up all the puddles by morning."

By the time we got home it was raining hard. And it felt kind of sticky outside. Dad came out to the driveway with an umbrella for Mom, and I just ran as fast as I could to the door. Austin was bouncing around in front of the door with his tongue hanging out like it always does during thunderstorms. I was surprised to see Ashton, Amber, and Ansley all curled up on the couch sound asleep.

"Why are the girls all out here in the living room?" Mom looked at Dad curiously.

"We were dancing in the kitchen to some music on the radio when a weather bulletin was announced. Didn't you hear anything about it? Severe storms are headed this way tonight and the girls started getting worried about the concert tomorrow. They just would not settle down so I said they could come sleep out here until Lena came home." Dad grinned a little and went into the kitchen with Mom to talk quietly while she got us a little snack to eat before bed. I was so hungry!

I went to my room and got my pajamas on, dropping my damp clothes in the middle of the floor. I would think about picking them up later.

When I got back into the kitchen Mom and Dad were on speakerphone, talking quietly with Mallory. I listened as she was talking. "We had to pull the bus over into a rest area because of the storms. I don't think I have ever seen it so windy, either! A huge branch came tumbling right across the front window after we parked."

"Hi, Mallory," I slipped in when she stopped talking a minute.

"Hey, Lena! How are you? How's Emma doing? Your parents were just filling me in."

I leaned on my dad and he put his arm around my shoulder. "Everything is okay here. I am getting a little nervous . . . a lot nervous. And now I don't know if Emma will be there to help out tomorrow. What will we do without her?" I knew I sounded like I was going to cry. "Are you going to be able to make it here to Dallas even with the storm, Mallory? What if you can't make it?" Thoughts of having to cancel the concert and not being able to raise any money for Caroline and the other children started crowding up in my brain.

"Oh, Lena! Who do we go to when we start having doubts or are getting scared?" I heard Mallory ask.

Dad squeezed me close to his side. "I know I go to God, and so does your mom."

"And so do I," Mallory put in. "So why don't we pray together right now? Maybe ask God for some help to stay safe in the storms, get some good sleep tonight, and for a beautiful and blessed day tomorrow? Mr. Daniels, do you mind praying for us?"

"Of course." Dad took a deep breath. "Dear God, thank you for friends and family and the time we have together. Bless each of us where we are tonight—Mallory and her crew as they make their way here to Dallas, our family as we settle in for the night in the storm, for Emma and her family as she recovers from her injury, and for the children that we are all working so hard to support from the children's hospital. Calm our fears, settle our minds, help us to remember that in You there is peace. In His name, amen."

We all said, "Amen," and smiled at each other just as a huge clap of lightning and thunder shook the house and a gusty wind made the front door come unlatched and swing open.

"We had better all get to bed soon. Tomorrow is going to be a busy day," Mom said, as she said goodbye to Mallory and walked out of the room to go close the door.

I yawned and said goodnight to Mallory too, and then Dad ended the call. I was feeling hungry but was just too tired to do anything about it and eat the snack Mom had put together, so I looked at Dad and closed my eyes pretending to fall asleep standing up. Just as he was gently guiding me out of the kitchen toward the bedroom hallway, we heard the weird sound of the severe weather siren outside.

"Dad! That means a big storm is close, doesn't it?" I said, panic in my voice. "What should we do?"

Mom walked toward us, already carrying Amber and guiding a very sleepy Ashton down the hall. "Get Ansley and their blankets and let's curl up in this inside hallway of the house. It's the safest place to be in a severe storm." She motioned Dad to the living room and me to follow her and the girls.

Dad also grabbed his phone and brought it with him so he could check weather bulletins as they were announced.

"Should we be scared?" Ansley whispered as she stuck her face in my armpit and snuggled up close.

"No. We are safe in the hall and God is protecting us."

"Okay, good," she mumbled and drifted back to sleep even with all the sirens and rain and wind outside.

As the family sat there together we heard some unfamiliar bumps and creaks. Austin didn't get too excited by the storm sounds. He just sat there panting and watching the hallway. When the lights flickered, he gave one tiny whine but then stood watch again. I petted his shaking body a little.

Dad sighed. "The weather reports are saying this is a severe thunderstorm. There haven't been any tornados

seen in the area! That is great news. Great news, for sure."
He smiled at Mom over Amber's head and leaned back
against the wall. "As soon as the sirens sound all clear, let's
get to bed."

Chapter 17

I had a hard time finally sleeping that night. I knew I really needed to, but I had so many things going through my mind. Was there any damage from the heavy rain and high winds at the school field? Would Mallory make it into Dallas? How was Emma? Was she still in pain? And the fear of not having her be a part of the event that she worked on so hard made me worry even more.

When my alarm rang the next morning, I struggled to wake up.

"Lena! Wake up!" Ansley shouted in my ear.

"Okay," I mumbled and tossed my covers over my head.

"Today's the day! It's the Big Event!"

I poked my head from under the blanket and corrected her, "The Big GIVE event."

"Well GEEET up!" Ansley tried to imitate me.

"I am. I am." I knew I needed to wake up.

When I walked into the kitchen I realized I was the last one to get up. Everyone else was wide awake with smiles on their faces.

"Why is everyone so happy?" I snapped a little.

Dad turned to me. "Do you not know what today is?" he said jokingly.

"I mean, what about the storm? And what about Emma? She worked so hard and now she can't even be there, can she?"

Mom stood up from the kitchen table and pulled me in close to her. "I talked to Emma's mom earlier this morning. Emma is okay. The doctors said she would not need surgery, just rest. So, let's thank God for that!"

I did feel a little relief after hearing the update on Emma but that didn't stop me from worrying about her not being at the concert.

Mom looked at my face and could tell that I was still feeling nervous. "As for the storm and any possible damage and clean up at school . . . we will deal with that if we have to. Dad and I already decided we should leave earlier than we planned, just in case there are a few things scattered around that were already outside. And honey, remember your Scripture! Do not be anxious about anything."

"So, stop worrying. God will work this out," Dad added. "Now! Get dressed! Remember we have to get there early for all of the deliveries too!"

I repeated Philippians 4:6 in my head while I showered and got ready for the big day. It was hard to believe that it was finally here.

"Girls, let's pray before we head to the school," Dad called out.

One by one, we hurried into the kitchen and gathered around the counter, holding hands.

"Can I pray, Daddy?" Amber asked.

Dad nodded and Amber prayed for our day.

When she finished, Dad pretended he was our coach and in his best coach voice he moved us out the door to the van and on our way.

While we were driving to school, it was plain to see

that there had been a pretty serious storm in the area last night. There were leaves and branches all over the place. Trashcans were tipped over and there was even lawn furniture and someone's trampoline in the middle of the road a little way from our house. We arrived at the school parking lot and I gasped.

"Oh, no!" I cried. "Look at that!"

One of the huge trees from the side of the field had been uprooted, the huge network of roots showing. It had fallen across the area where we had planned on setting up the T-shirt tent. And that wasn't all.

"Is that part of the gym roof?" Mom said, pointing in the direction of a huge sheet of what looked like metal in the middle of the field. It was bent up almost in half but was huge! "I've never seen anything like that," she said softly and shook her head.

Dad parked the van and we all hopped out. I ran toward the small group of people that was already gathering, including Mr. Fraser and Ms. Blount. They were all calmly discussing next steps to take. As Mom and Dad joined us I noticed a big white truck with the local TV station's call letters painted on the side with a large satellite tower folded down up on top. A woman in a blue suit jumped out and came toward us.

"Hi, folks. I'm Annette Courtier from WDDD, channel 13 news. We've been getting calls all morning about the storm damage in the area and someone tipped us off that you may be in need of some assistance. What's going on here?" the young woman asked no one in particular.

Mom nudged me forward and I smiled at everyone and

jumped right in. "Well, my name is Lena Daniels and I go to school here. My friends and I planned a big fundraiser for tonight—The Big Give—maybe you've heard about it? Mallory Winston is actually going to be here to sing live tonight!" I took a breath. "Anyway, as you can see, the field where the concert is supposed to be is a huge mess. We were all just talking about what to do."

Ms. Blount stepped up and added, "I am the teacher that is helping the girls with the fundraiser—Ms. Blount." She shook hands with the reporter. "I think you most certainly can help us! We need as many hands as we can get to help clean up the debris from the field—especially the roofing pieces and the tree. And we need to get this all done soon. Tents, a stage, and many donations are on their way. Can you do a small live piece for the early morning news? As soon as possible? I watch you every Saturday . . ." Ms. Blount smiled again. "If you mention the cause it may get people from the neighborhood to come by and offer some help. Do you think it could work?"

I was jumping for joy inside. What a great idea! And maybe more people would hear about the event this way and want to come to the concert too. Or at least buy a T-shirt or donate some money.

I ran up to Ms. Blount and surprised her with a hug. "What a great idea!" Ms. Blount patted my back as she hugged me back just as Savannah and Joey came running up.

Everyone laughed as Annette Courtier nodded and walked away to talk with her camera crew.

She got everything set up very quickly, the satellite tower raised slowly into the air. And the report went live.

"This is Annette Courtier with WDDD News, and I am here at a local middle school where a fundraiser called The Big Give is being held tonight—but folks, they need your help! First, let's have Lena Daniels and the rest of the organizers say a few words about the event. Lena?"

I felt very comfortable being in front of the camera. It wasn't like *Above the Waters,* and it wasn't like the tour with Mallory either. But I knew I had a message and I had to get it out to people. "My friends and I planned a big benefit concert for tonight, featuring Mallory Winston. But look around us! The storm and winds that went through last night really messed our field up. We need to be success-ful since we are raising money so that five children from Peru can stay in the United States and get the medical treat-ments they need. The hospital they were at is closing . . . Anyway, please, if you can come here to help us clean up, it would be great!"

Joey spoke up, "And then you can buy a ticket and go to a really great concert too, while you're here!"

The reporter chuckled. "So there you have it, folks! If you want to help a great cause and then have some fun while you're at it, please come . . ." She closed her live report with the location of the school and a comment about bring-ing work gloves, trash bags, and a chainsaw or two to help with the tree. "That's a wrap!" she said as she smiled at our group and wished us the best.

"You are doing a great thing here, girls. Where can I get a ticket? I think I'd like to come back later for the show."

Mr. Fraser walked over to take her into school, where he could get her a ticket. And Savannah, Joey, and I looked

at each other and fell into a group hug. We were all kind of
in shock. So much was going on.

"I can't believe it!" Savannah shouted and cheered all
at the same time. Joey just kept jumping and clapping and
I was doing a combination of them both. "It's finally here
and look at this place. There was hardly even any rain by
my house! And it looks like it was bad here!"

I nodded. "This side of town was really hit. I just
hope the news report gets some volunteers here to help us
clean up."

"Has anyone heard from Emma?" Joey asked as she
kicked at rocks on the ground, knocking them into a small
puddle.

"Well, Mom said she's going to be okay. She didn't need
surgery or anything. But I feel so bad for her."

"Me too," said Savannah.

We stood there quietly for a moment, trying to move
on. We all knew we had to get busy with or without our
missing friend.

And get busy we did! It was not long after the live news
report that we started noticing more and more people
showing up at the school field. God was sending us help . . .
we only had to trust Him! Dad and Mom were so right.
Soon everywhere we looked volunteers were picking up
leaves, sticks, and trash that had blown into the field over-
night. The big piece of roofing hadn't been from the school
after all, but from a building down the road, and that was
being moved into a large dumpster so that it was out of the
way. There was a loud whine from a couple of chainsaws
that were cutting up the tree on the side of the field, and we

could hear the beep-beep of a couple of trucks backing in to drop off donations like the tents, food, chairs and tables, and so much more! Everyone was moving so fast it was hard to know exactly what was happening.

As the day progressed, the field began to fill with the parent and student volunteers that had signed up before the storm too. Ms. Blount, Mr. Fraser, and Mr. Shipply were there, guiding and organizing people. Ms. Blount was even wearing one of the shirts with a pair of dark blue jeans. It was fun to see her in something different than her long flowery skirts, but I liked it.

When someone would ask where things needed to go Savannah, Joey, and I would look at our clipboards and point them in the right direction. If someone needed a cord, directions to the restroom, or had a question we would jump right in and take care of it. It felt weird to have so many people asking us to show them what to do but it also made me feel very grateful. All our planning was starting to pay off. Things seemed to be going without a hitch.

I was kneeling down at one of the tables, helping Mr. Shipply look for a note he had dropped, when I heard Joey screaming my name.

"Lena! Lena!"

I stepped out of the tent and saw her running toward me. "She's here!! She's here!"

"Emma?!" I started moving quickly in her direction.

Joey slowed down. "Oh, no. Sorry. No, Emma is not here. Mallory is!"

"Ohhh!" I giggled a little and followed Joey. Mallory was standing in the parking lot near her bus, unloading her bags. She dropped everything when she saw me coming and reached out to hug me.

"Hey, girl!" she said. I told her how happy I was to see her and introduced her to Joey. Joey managed to stop giggling long enough to say, "Hello."

We helped Mallory carry her things to the field and stopped along the way to let her say hi to my family and Savannah. When we heard the sound guy calling her name from the stage that her crew had already set up, we showed her where to go for her sound check.

As soon as she could no longer see us, my sisters and friends started jumping and screaming. I couldn't believe she was here and our event was actually going to happen!

"Lena!"

I heard someone calling my name but I could not remember where I recognized the voice from. I turned to see who it was and screamed louder than before, "KAY B!"

I jumped into her arms and wrapped myself around her. I had not seen Kay B since the movie premiere. Savannah immediately remembered her and ran over to say hi too.

"How did you know about today?" I asked.

Kay B pointed her finger in my mother's direction and waved. "So, how can I help? I am absolutely all yours. Tell me what needs to be done, kiddos, and I'll get busy!" And she immediately jumped right in with helping to set up the tables and chairs in the tents. She also made a few jokes about needing to get us to our places on time like she did while we had been filming.

From the middle of the field I turned in a full circle and looked around. I could hear Mallory practicing, I could see

Kay B working alongside my family, my teachers, and my friends. Everyone was wearing their colored shirts and I knew today was going to be one of the best days ever! Nothing—not my fears or even a severe storm could ruin this day and this event!

Crowds and crowds of people were lining up along the side of the field that had been roped off as the entrance to The Big Give. Everyone was in a great mood. There were shouts of hello to friends and cheers when others heard Mallory sound-checking. Volunteers in the tent selling and distributing T-shirts were kept busy from the minute they started letting people onto the field. And the food booths selling hotdogs and drinks had lines out the tent entrance.

"One hour until show time!" Mr. Fraser's loud voice boomed from the stage.

I let out one loud "EECKKKKKK!!" and went to find Savannah and Joey.

Chapter 18

I hustled across the field to the main tent and headed for the T-shirt table, and I could not believe my eyes.

Emma was sitting behind the table in a wheelchair with her leg pointed straight out on a support.

"Hey," she said casually, trying not to laugh.

"EMMA!" I cried.

"Now you didn't think I could miss The Big Give, did you?" Her smile was so bright—she was glowing.

Tears started to stream down my cheeks. I was so happy to see her. Ashton and Amber ran off to tell Joey and Savannah the news. They all came running to the table to greet Emma too.

After we finished celebrating that Emma was back, Joey blurted out, "Uh-oh! Who is going to host the show?"

My heart started to beat really fast, and my head was spinning. We were so worried about Emma and busy cleaning and setting up that we completely forgot Emma was our host. I looked at her in her chair and knew there was no way she could still do it up on stage.

I knew that it would be hard for me to host the event, sign autographs, and share my story while trying to make sure that everything was running smoothly with the whole program.

"What are we going to do?" I cried out.

Ms. Blount overheard us and joined our circle. "Don't panic. Savannah can do it."

"Okay, okay, let's not get too excited about that idea. I can't do it, but Joey can," Savannah said.

Joey gasped. "I could but then who is going to stay out in the crowds and help people?"

Savannah looked sick. I knew the thought of her hanging out with people in the crowd was just as scary for her as being on stage.

I walked over to her, grabbed her hands, and looked her in the face. Savannah had always been the one to encourage me to step outside of my comfort zone and now it was my turn to return the favor.

"Savannah, remember how scared I was about going to LA to film the movie?"

She nodded.

". . . and about hosting the premiere and about going on tour and signing autographs and talking to strangers . . . ?" Savannah continued to nod her head slowly and stare at me.

"You can do this! God wants you to step out of your comfort zone so that others will see Him shine in you!"

Savannah grabbed her stomach and hunched over a little. We all stood there, anticipating her response.

"Twenty minutes until the show must start, girls!" Mr. Fraser whisked by and warned us.

"Okay. Okay. I can do it. I think. Okay, yes, yes, I can. Oh, no . . . okay yes. Just pray. I got it."

"Yes, you do!" Joey cheered and everyone around us joined in.

I walked Savannah over to the stage and went over

every detail of the program with her. I asked Mallory to pray for her like she always did for me before a show when we were on tour. After we prayed, Savannah and I stood holding hands as the crowd began to settle down in front of the stage. There were so many people! Seeing so many different colored shirts made me happy!

I wasn't sure where all the time had gone but the sun was starting to set and I knew we were just seconds away from making The Big Give become a reality.

Mr. Fraser came over and looked at Savannah. "They are ready for you!"

Savannah squeezed my hand tighter. I reached down with my other hand and peeled her fingers away from mine. "GO, GO, GO!" I cheered and nudged her onto the stage.

I was excited to watch Savannah be so courageous and fun. She held the microphone tightly as she introduced herself and welcomed everyone to the concert.

"This has been a real adventure for us. What started out as a way to help some children get needed medical treatment at a new hospital has turned into this huge event! We even get to hear Mallory Winston sing live, people!"

Then she called me out to the stage to share my story and introduce Mallory. "But before we hear Mallory, let's meet my best friend and the girl who started this whole benefit—Lena Daniels!"

I ran out and hugged her before I started talking. I was so proud of Savannah that I did not even think about being nervous for myself.

While I was talking, pictures of Caroline and the other kids were playing on a huge screen behind me. I turned slightly and saw some of them and started to cry. "As soon as I read the card that Mallory sent me, I just knew I had to do something to help Caroline and her friends at the hospital, and here we are today. It's The Big Give! I am so thankful that you have all joined in the fun and are helping these great kids to get better!" When I was done, I asked everyone to give their loudest scream to welcome Mallory to the stage.

Everyone was screaming and her music started playing! She ran out on stage full of energy and waving hello to the crowd. I gave her a high-five and turned to leave the stage but I felt her grab my arm.

"Hold on there, Lena Daniels! We have a surprise for you, your sisters, and Savannah, Joey, and Emma."

I stopped in my tracks and turned back toward the crowd very slowly.

We waited while Joey and Savannah walked up on stage with Emma holding herself up on each of their shoulders. Amber, Ansley, and Ashton scrambled to the front of the stage so that we could see them.

Mallory spoke into her microphone, "Lena, I love seeing how God is using you and how you have come up with a way to let your light shine for so many others to see. The first time you were up on a stage you were so nervous and now, here you are, pulling everyone else onto the stage with you! I just want to take a moment to celebrate you and your awesome friends for putting this event together! I am so grateful that God made each of you! And each of YOU!" Mallory pointed out to the audience. So many of the volunteers from the morning storm cleanup had stayed for

the concert too. "I hear the field was a mess from the storm and it looks amazing out there! Thanks to you!!"

There were shouts, screams, and applause. It was louder than the thunder from last night's storms!

"Now, Lena, one more thing . . . there are some people that want to thank you."

From the corner of my eye I could see a small group walking toward me, across the stage. As they got closer I recognized Caroline and two other kids.

I dropped to my knees and started crying. I could not believe my eyes. Mallory reached down and pulled me back up to my feet.

Caroline was walking slowly and I couldn't wait to hug her. I tried not to squeeze her too hard but I was so emotional I could not help myself.

Mallory gave us a few moments to cry and smile before she said, "Okay, there's one more thing before we get this show really started! Watch this."

"Lena Daniels," Mr. Fenway's face appeared on the screen behind me. I could not believe it! "Hi, there," he said once I was facing him. "And hello to everyone!"

"We are so sorry we could not be right there with you today but when Mallory told us about what you were doing for these sweet families, we knew we wanted to help too. So, Caroline, we have sent a donation for you and your friends."

Kay B walked out on stage holding a white envelope and handed it to me.

"This is our gift to your families."

Caroline smiled and waved a little at the screen and Mr. Fenway.

"Lena, and all of you girls, keep shining! The whole world needs to see your light. And we will be watching!"

The crowd started cheering again, and Mallory was clapping and jumping.

She spun around to the crowd and shouted, "Are y'all ready to celebrate? Who is ready to hear some music?!"

I couldn't help but join in with the crowd and shout, "YEAH!"

We all walked off stage and found our way back to the audience and spots near our families in the front, to join in enjoying all our hard work.

After the concert, Mallory and I sat behind a table signing T-shirts, arms, posters, and anything else that people wanted. I loved every minute of it but when the crowds finally started to leave I was sort of glad. I was exhausted.

We stayed around for a long while after the music was over and the crowds had all gone home. We all had to pitch in and help clean up and pack things away. Eventually, Dad came to find me to let me know that we were just about ready to go.

Mr. Fraser, Ms. Blount, and Mr. Shipply were walking with him and Mom.

"You ladies ready to go?" he asked.

Savannah and Joey were sprawled across a grassy patch in the middle of the field. Emma was resting in her wheelchair with her leg up, and I was sitting with my legs crossed, Amber on my lap. Ansley and Ashton were each sitting at my side, dozing off in the night air.

"Well, before you go, I wanted to let you know that this is what we call a sold-out show. Between the ticket sales, the extra T-shirts we sold, the food and drinks we sold, and additional monetary donations, you ladies raised about $105,000 dollars!"

"WOAH!!!" Joey exclaimed.

"That's amazing!" I said before remembering the white envelope Kay B had handed us earlier in the evening. I reached to my side and pulled it from my clipboard. I waved it in the air before opening it.

"From the Fenway's, remember?" I said.

I gently ripped the envelope open and it fell to the ground. I held up the check and jumped straight to my feet. "$50,000!" I screamed.

"What?" Mom and Dad shouted in shock. They reached for it and were just as amazed as I was. None of us could believe our eyes.

"That makes the total raised $155,000! I can't believe it! That's $5,000 more than our goal!"

"These families are going to be able to stay! All of them!" Mom raised both of her hands in the air and started thanking God.

I looked around at everyone celebrating and crying. It felt like a dream.

The great thing is, I wasn't dreaming. This was all happening and this was my real life.

"You girls did it!" Ms. Blount looked at us and smiled. Before I could reply, Joey did.

"Nope! God did it!"

Mom started crying harder. I hugged each of my friend's necks and my sisters wrapped themselves around our legs.

I pulled my head back from the circle and looked up

at the sky. There were just a few stars twinkling but they were all I could see. I leaned forward again and heard my friends sniffling. I whispered loud enough for us all to hear, "Thank you, God."

Lena in the Spotlight

Alena Pitts with Wynter Pitts

Hello Stars

Hello Stars introduces Lena Daniels, a Headstrong and determined girl, who has her life planned out to the minute. When Lena unexpectedly lands a movie role, is it too good to be true? This spirited 11-year-old must find a way to balance stardom with "real" life. Suddenly Lena wishes she had time for her three younger sisters and her friends. Find out what happens in *Hello Stars*!

Read this excerpt from
Hello Stars, book one in the
Lena in the Spotlight series,
where Lena's adventures all began!

Hello Stars

Chapter 1

"Mom, don't forget to let Austin out today," I yelled back through the two glass kitchen doors. Austin was still standing there, watching as Amber and I were the first to head out for the day.

I kept thinking about him and how badly I wished he could come to school with me. I once asked my science teacher, Mr. Lipscomb, if we could use him as a class pet but the idea was quickly rejected when he realized Austin doesn't like to sit still, partially follows rules, and sometimes nibbles on chairs. But how awesome would school be if he could be there? Totally awesome.

Oh, Austin is my wrinkle-faced, floppy eared, four-legged friend. Technically he's a blue-nosed bully puppy but he's much more human than any dog I have ever met.

"Just twenty-eight days left, boy!" I yelled louder to get him excited.

Dad flung the doors open with Ansley and Ashton hurrying behind him.

"Love you, Mom!"

Austin scurried away and my sisters and I followed Dad and headed to the van.

"Twenty-eight days till what, Lena?" Amber asked.

"That's how many days I have left in the fifth grade! Then it's summer vacation and I can't wait!"

Amber took the news and chased behind Dad calling his name until she reached his side.

She reached him right before he slid the back door open. She wrapped her tiny arms around his khaki pant leg and exclaimed, "It's almost summer!"

One-by-one we tossed our book bags, lunchboxes, and water bottles in and hopped into the back of our minivan.

"I wanted to tell you I have to go out of town today. It's a quick trip so I won't be home this evening, but I'll see you in time for school tomorrow morning, ok?"

"Ok!" we responded in unison.

Ansley used the short car ride to school to discuss her upcoming ninth birthday plans, while Ashton and Amber sat in the back talking about how excited they were to be graduating from kindergarten in just a few weeks.

"Ok, here we are." Dad's announcement caused everyone to pause their conversations.

I glanced down at my watch. The digits 8:12 flashed before my eyes.

"We only have three minutes! I don't want to be late today."

Dad pulled his car forward until we reached the main school doors. They were already swinging shut.

Dad let out a deep grunt. "Sorry guys. Love you!"

"Love you too, Daddy!" we yelled as we hopped out of the van and headed into the big brick building.

Ansley ran to the left, Amber and Ashton to the right, and I raced straight ahead to Ms. Blount's history class. I whispered a silent prayer, *"Dear God, please let her door still be open."*

I hated being late to Ms. Blount's class. She's my history and language arts teacher. She also happens to be a huge rule follower. So if her door was closed then I would most definitely need to get a tardy pass from the office. Which meant that I would be even later to class than I already was.

Unfortunately, when I reached room 109, the door was closed.

I carefully stood on my tiptoes to peek through the skinny glass window next to the door. I wanted to see inside without Ms. Blount seeing or hearing me. Everyone was shuffling around in their backpacks and shoving loose papers into their notebooks. I waited until my eyes met Savannah's. She flashed a sheepish grin in my direction and quickly looked away.

Savannah is always on time and prepared. I remember meeting her in the first grade. When I walked into the classroom she was sitting straight against the back of her chair, her feet placed perfectly side-by-side in front her, and she had on a pair of white ruffled socks that matched the two large white hair bows dangling from each side of her head. Her hands were crossed delicately, resting on top of her desk. She looked perfect and I knew right away we would become the best of friends.

I dropped back down to my heels and exhaled. I marched to the office and filled out the tardy sheet. I crumbled the pink copy with the faded words and stuffed it into my backpack. I balled the white copy up in my left fist and marched right back up to room 109. I knocked on the door, held up the crinkled copy of the white excuse sheet and smiled. Ms. Blount opened the door and welcomed me in.

"Good morning, Ms. Blount," I said apologetically.

"Good morning," she replied without ever moving her actual mouth. I'm always amazed at how she does that. No expression. No smile. No eye contact. Just a gravelly voice that escapes a tiny hole between her top and bottom lips.

I handed her the paper as quickly as I could and slid past her through the door and into the room. I spotted my empty chair right next to Savannah, so I headed in that direction to take my place.

As I walked past Savannah's desk, I nodded and mouthed, "How'd it go?" She knew I was talking about her weekend at our favorite singer Mallory Winston's concert, so she gave me a *can't wait to tell you about it, but not now* thumbs up and finished coloring in the pattern of funny faces she had already drawn all over her worksheet.

Great, I thought to myself.

Ms. Blount was in the middle of explaining how George Washington had never really cut down a cherry tree.

I put on my glasses, opened my eyes really wide, and tried to focus.

For some reason it wasn't working. I just couldn't seem to stop my brain from drifting into a magical world full of baby Austins swimming in pools of cherry flavored whipped cream clouds surrounded by rainbows and puppy treats.

Before I knew it, half the day was over and everyone was grabbing their things and heading to lunch.

"I'm starving! Let's find Emma," Savannah announced as we strolled toward the cafeteria.

Savannah and I scanned the large room until we spotted

Emma in the middle of a huge crowd. She was wearing her knee-high white lace socks, her navy uniform skirt with the two large red buttons on the front, and she had her black fringed vest tossed on over her white uniform shirt.

Emma burst through the crowd chanting, "Lena! Lena! Savannah! Hey, over here!"

"Hey, girl!" Savannah wrapped her arms around Emma's neck. "Love the socks."

"Me too. But wait until Ms. Blount sees them! You're gonna get it!" I sneered playfully.

"Wait—what's wrong with these?" Emma seemed genuinely surprised by my warning as she knocked her knees together and shrugged innocently.

I have never been able to figure out how she can get away with being completely out of uniform every day, but she does. It's probably because Emma knows how to make everyone smile with her silly jokes and spunky smile. She is always ready to have fun and I think even the overly strict teachers like Ms. Blount appreciate that.

Savannah and I followed Emma to a table mostly full of friends from her homeroom. This is the first year since first grade that the three of us haven't shared a single class together. We missed her but our friendship is strong enough to survive a few hours apart.

Emma slid into the open space between two of her friends while Savannah and I sat directly across from them. Deliberately and quietly everyone emptied their lunch bags. I reached into my right pocket and pulled out my sandwich. Then I reached into my left and grabbed a handful of snacks.

"Still no lunchbox?" Savannah asked

"Nope, and I'm not ready to tell my mom yet. Anyone want my fruit snacks?" I waved the little blue bag from side-to-side in the air.

"Oooo, I'll take them!" Emma reached across the table to grab them but I pulled them back just in time for her hand to land on top of my already smooshed sandwich. We all burst out laughing.

I put my finger over my open mouth and whispered "shhh," through my giggles. I could feel Ms. Blount glaring in our direction and I didn't want anyone to get in trouble.

"Hurry and eat guys, so we can go outside. We have a lot to talk about!" Savannah urged.

"Oooo, I almost forgot!" Emma practically screamed.

"You went to Mallory Winston's concert! Did you get to meet her? Which songs did she sing?" Emma tossed question after question out to Savannah. Savannah caught each of them and calculated her thoughts before offering any responses. Emma and I were sitting on the edge of our seats filled with anticipation.

Savannah's grandmother had given her two tickets for her birthday. Emma and I were pretty sad that we didn't get to go with her but we didn't think it would be fair for her to choose just one of us, so we all agreed it would be best if she took her cousin instead. At least one of us got to go. All we needed was for her to tell us all about it!

"She'll fill us in after lunch," I said quietly to try and calm Emma down a bit.

I could see Ms. Blount moving toward our table.

"Uh-oh."

Her steps were long and slow until she was standing

in the small space between my back and the fourth grade table behind me.

I stuffed a few green grapes into my mouth. Savannah took a gulp from her orange water bottle while Emma continued to talk.

"Savannah, I can't wait! Please tell me now!"

"Lena Daniels," Ms. Blount spoke sternly.

I wasn't even talking, I thought to myself.

I spun around but in slow motion.

"Yes, ma'am?" I whimpered in a voice of total fear and complete panic.

"Mr. Lipscomb would like to see you in the science room," she said. "Finish your lunch and go straight there. You can head right to recess after."

I said a quick "yes, ma'am," and turned back around. I took the last bite of my sandwich and jumped up from the table.

"Don't say anything about Mallory until I get back!"

I doubled my normal walking speed as I headed to Mr. Lipscomb's room.

He greeted me at the door and his first words were, "Tomorrow is dissection day—"

From there, I knew exactly what he wanted. Mr. Lipscomb always calls on me when he needs help in the science lab. He says I am responsible. He wanted me to clean the tables before the dissection the next day. I asked him why we cleaned the tables before if it was just going to get covered in slime, blood, and animal guts. He said it needed to be sanitary for the animals. I didn't understand this either. Why do we make it sanitary for a *dead* animal?

I am 99% sure the animal doesn't have feelings. And if it did, I'm pretty sure he or she was going to care a lot more about getting cut open and pulled apart than the table being cleaned for its second death.

But, oh well. I finished our conversation with "yes, sir, I can do it" and headed to recess.

Emma and Savannah ran toward me. "Lena! Lena! Hurry up!!!" they yelled.

Savannah did not waste any time before jumping right into all the fascinating Mallory Winston details we had been waiting to hear all morning.

"The concert was fabulous!"

Emma raised her hands in the air and wiggled her wrists, causing her hands to flail uncontrollably.

Savannah continued, "She was wearing purple boots! And she had a purple feather in her hair to match!"

"That's so cool!" Emma screeched.

"I want a pair," I said softly.

I am pretty sure Savannah didn't hear either of us. She was so excited that she just kept right on talking. It was so fun seeing her this energetic and full of spunk. Not many things can pull this much enthusiasm from Savannah but Mallory Winston had a way of making us all smile.

"When she first came on stage she was alone with just one tiny light shining on her. She was holding her guitar and guess what she sang?" Savannah asked but we all knew she didn't need an answer.

She had our full attention. We stood directly in front of her, captivated by each word she spoke.

"Lena, she sang "Run Away with Me"!"

I bent my knees and pushed my body downward play-fully until I was almost on the ground.

Savannah reached down and pretended to catch me. "Don't worry. We recorded it for you. I'll show you the next time you come over!"

"Yay!" I cheered.

Savannah's eyes grew as big as ping-pong balls and she leaned forward. "You guys are not going to believe this . . . it's the best part—Mallory Winston is having a contest! It's like a chance to audition for a movie. But guess what the best part is?"

"What??" The anticipation was building and I could feel my heart doing a happy dance inside my chest.

"The winner will get to meet her! You and Emma have to do it! This is your chance to meet Mallory Winston!"

The three of us became one big ball of bouncy noise.

"Wait, but how?" Emma said exactly what I was thinking.

"She said the information is on her website. Just go to it and enter!"

We all jumped up and down again.

"Savannah, you have to do it too!" I demanded even though I already knew she probably wouldn't. She's way too shy for that.

The bell rang and we darted in separate directions.

"Bye, Emma!" Savannah and I called as we headed inside and back towards Room 109.

When Ms. Blount announced we had earned a little reward time for finishing our grammar worksheets on time, I knew exactly what I wanted to do. I needed to tell someone about my chance to meet Mallory! I found the huge blue beanbag in the back corner of our classroom under the huge wooden frame we made as a class. It looked like a window full of stars in the middle of the wall. We'd each signed our names on a little star and placed them on a huge piece of dark blue construction paper behind the frame. Ms. Blount said she wanted us to always remember to shine.

I opened the little black notebook I had recently gotten for my eleventh birthday, and started writing.

Hello, Stars,

Today is the best day ever! You know that Mallory Winston concert that Savannah went to? Well, she just told us all about it and that there's a chance I could actually meet her!! That would be the best thing ever! I'm gonna pray and ask God to make that happen. Mallory loves God and I love her, so I hope He listens!

Dear God,

Can you help me to meet Mallory Winston? Ok, thanks!

For the rest of the day my head was spinning with the thought of meeting Mallory Winston. Even though I had no idea what I needed to do, I was determined that I would do it as soon as I got home.

Day Dreams and Movie Screens

Eleven-year-old Lena Daniels' summer of Hollywood starlets and movie filming alongside her favorite singer, Mallory Winston, is over. School will be back in full swing, and it seems as though life might just pick up where it left off—with volleyball games, homework, and her best friends.

But just as she begins to wonder if her summer was all just a dream, her world is turned upside down . . . again! The movie premiers, the previews seem to be splattered on every television and radio channel, and everyone knows her name. Her classmates, strangers, and even her friends are starting to treat her differently, and everywhere she turns she's being asked for an autograph, a picture, or a hug.

Lena is just figuring out how to manage her new fame at home when she finds out she's hitting the road on a two-week bus tour to further promote the film. Traveling across the country with the cast—with the surprise addition of her whole family joining them—Lena experiences adventures and challenges she never expected, while learning to step outside of her comfort zone and follow the path God has for her life. She learns that saying yes to God may not always be easy, but will take her further than she ever imagined!

Available in stores and online!

Connect with Faithgirlz!

 http://www.faithgirlz.com/

 www.facebook.com/Faithgirlz/

www.instagram.com/zonderkidz_faithgirlz/

twitter.com/zonderkidz?lang=en/

www.pinterest.com/zkidzfaithgirlz/